The Hunger
of Women

The Hunger
of Women

Marosia Castaldi

*Translated from the
Italian by Jamie Richards*

SHEFFIELD – LONDON – NEW YORK

First published in English in 2023 by And Other Stories
Sheffield – London – New York
www.andotherstories.org

Copyright © Piero Manni s.r.l. 2012.
Originally published in Italian as *La fame delle donne* in 2012.

Translation copyright © Jamie Richards, 2023

1 3 5 7 9 8 6 4 2

ISBN: 9781913505868
eBook ISBN: 9781913505875

Editor: Jeremy M. Davies; Copy-editor: Bella Bosworth; Proofreader:
Maddie Rogers; Typesetter: Tetragon, London; Typefaces: Albertan Pro and
Linotype Syntax (interior) and Stellage (cover); Series Cover Design: Elisa von
Randow, Alles Blau Studio, Brazil, after a concept by And Other Stories.

And Other Stories books are printed and bound in the UK on FSC-certified paper by
the CPI Group (UK) Ltd, Croydon. The covers are of G . F Smith 270gsm Colorplan
card – made in the Lake District at the environmentally friendly James Cropper
paper mill – and are embossed with biodegradable foils from FoilCo, Warrington.

A catalogue record for this book is available from the British Library.

And Other Stories gratefully acknowledge that our work is
supported using public funding by Arts Council England.

This book is a co-production with the Italian Cultural Institute in
London and was made possible by a special funding of the Italian
Ministry of Foreign Affairs and International Cooperation.

1

A woman in a standalone house ran the vacuum every morning I saw my life reflected in her lot Like her I spent my time cleaning and cooking for my family I had a grown daughter who still lived at home It was just us two but we were a family I was a widow I gave her my recipes My husband died in a car accident He was in the hospital for a long time I spent sleepless nights beside him as he succumbed He fell into a coma and I made the momentous decision to pull the plug Since then the wisdom of the ages has nestled in my memory I kept photos from the happy times when we would go to the country house that we later sold I talked about him to the neighbor woman with whom I shared recipes like eggplant parmesan You slice the eggplant fry it in oil bake it with tomato sauce parmesan and mozzarella

Sometimes she ventured to imitate my recipes We had intimate dinners we three lone women She looked into our eyes She spoke little Like me she'd broken away from society When I went to eat at her place I'd bring homemade pasta and bread to her table and we'd light candles for us three lone women My daughter didn't always come She said the neighbor and I were like a couple of war widows Our problem was living in anxiety or abandonment Solitude corrodes the soul—Reader—

We three lone women would visit at dinner and the neighbor would tell us about the housewares store she used to have She would spend hours arranging coffee pots and salad bowls in the window She'd put all her savings in that business after her husband died The neighbors commended her hard work and goodwill Everyone in the little town where we lived remembered her shop She had a boundless love for objects which gave her refuge like an open shore after a storm That's where she got the vacuum that now she used at home

The sound of that vacuum that she used maniacally was a savage drone that dispelled sleep and peace Maniacally she cleaned the whole house every day Nothing was ever clean enough She looked around The dust of time was her nemesis Ravenous time snapped at her ankles

The sound of the vacuum was a deafening drone that blasted like a storm wind into the houses of our little hilltop town that held the wisdom of the ages in its ancient earth Every window had a grille with a clock and a copper pot and a worn doily Everything exuded oldness Everyone knew everyone's business They talked about those three lone women who had the audacity to engage in trade and commerce on their own They cursed the din that vacuum made growling night and day like a chained animal They were driven mad by the deafening tick-tock of clocks that mark the tempo of death and life The neighbor's husband had been a butcher who worked day and night preparing stuffed chickens and liver roulades and roasted veal with bay thyme sage rosemary the smells of which wafted from the shop They made fifty-person dinners to order in their rich little town in the Po Lowlands full of fog and crime in winter when everyone holed up away from the cold and damp and sad nights Incest theft violence multiplied They kept a gun in the drawer

The neighbor devoted herself to dusting the terracotta and porcelain knickknacks left over from running the shop all those years She'd painted the walls in blue and white stripes All the neighbor ladies were jealous and gossiped about her She was still young at the time They said she'd gotten the money for her shop ingratiating herself like a whore with a wealthy local entrepreneur who owned a confectionary Every day they saw him bring a box of sweets to the widow who bared her fair fleshy arms She'd put on weight since her husband's death A good meal was all she wanted after a day's work Lustily and lazily she ate the man's sweets while the neighbors' tongues wagged

The store was blue and white and bright When it was quiet the neighbor peeked out at the street and the oaks and the alders on the lane Everyone in town came to her for wedding and baptism and confirmation favors The coffee pots the cups the glasses exposed to the sun their bare skin from which the dust of time had been lifted by the shopkeeper's hands that dusted them daily The dust of time, time was her sworn enemy At home and in the store she silenced every irksome tick every shrieking alarm The madness of clocks would be the death of her

She looked around her and found refuge in a sandwich or dessert that subdued her yearning for love and affection I gave her the recipes of my dead mother whom I'd seen in her white shroud Before she died I brought her pastina with fresh tomato sauce You take cherry tomatoes on the vine sauté them and strain them then add a little salt sugar and oil and basil no garlic and pour the hot sauce over pasta al dente

I gave her my mother's recipe for pastry dough You combine flour with equal parts butter and sugar Knead the dough into a dense grainy ball and place it under a cloth to rest after carving a cross in the top Roll it out on a board then place it in molds with fruit and pastry cream and glaze Then bake it at medium heat for thirty minutes

The shopkeeper tried to cook but she wasn't very good Her true talent was cleaning

After the housewares store she got bored and replaced the knickknacks with shoes The empty shoes watched the road like strongholds of time They were empty of themselves as if waiting to be filled with the warmth of a foot They contained the same enigma as the shoes in the Edita Broglio painting that depicts them like the virgins waiting with their lamps and oil for the time when we'll all leave this earth Maniacally she dusted the shoes and tried them on her plump glutton feet She gave me some red shoes like a pair my mother had bought me when I was a little girl In return I gave her my recipe for shortcrust You mix flour water oil and salt into a silky dough by rolling it out and kneading it until it's springy Then roll it out over a large surface into a big layer that you cut and put on baking sheets to make savory pies with meat and vegetables You bake them on medium heat until the crust turns golden These dishes are full of the Mediterranean wisdom of the ages that my mother passed down to me When we were little smells from the kitchen wafted through our old house like indelible traces of what had been *Be calm* my soul's voice says when my mind returns to my noble mother's chapped white hands consumed by the extreme domesticitude that corroded her life Only by passing down her love for making food that her mother had passed down to her did she find a crumb of eternity on this earth

I taught the neighbor simple things like bread with butter and tuna or butter and sugar and bread with oil tomatoes and salt and Neapolitan caponata which you make by soaking a frisella in water and topping it with chopped tomato mozzarella oregano salt and oil Those heavenly hunks of bread are the taste of childhood I also gave her my recipe for stuffed peppers You peel roasted peppers and fill them with pasta olives and tomato sauce or with oil-soaked old bread capers parmesan parsley and olives You arrange them on a baking sheet and sprinkle them with breadcrumbs

One evening when I invited her to dinner she greedily ate four stuffed peppers It was a joyful hunger My daughter looked on in astonishment It was a joy to watch her as warmed by wine we drank our coffee She told us about her shoes enumerating them like children The shoe shop shone throughout the land

My daughter had no interest in housekeeping or cooking After working my whole life I lived off of interest from savings I'd put away in the bank I didn't look back I didn't want any nostalgia or bitterness

While we were having dinner I started thinking about a trip to the sea we could take together and as we ate I saw my dead mother's eyes that held centuries of Mediterranean wisdom My mother died thirty years ago consumed by the plague of our time that confined her to bed for nine months long enough to give birth to her death and her life and go to the land of no return where she would find my dead brother The lands of the Nevermore are invisible to the eyes of the living but appear in the wisdom of madness and delirium We ate foods made from her recipes that interested my daughter as little as housekeeping We ate fried anchovies You coat rinsed anchovies in flour and fry them in boiling salted oil You can also marinate them raw with salt parsley lemon and oil As my neighbor devoured the fish I told her about my mother's escarole pie and her other savory pies In the kitchen that was her life's prison and salvation my mother made bread by combining flour yeast water a pinch of salt and oil She kneaded the mixture into a dense and stretchy ball that she left to rise under a cloth in a warm place for an hour after carving into the raw dough the sign of the cross that was on the missal and the prayer book that she kept in the credenza that's now in my house and filled with her bills her recipes and her jewelry as if the recipes were as precious as gold She passed down to me the wisdom of the recipes that earned her a scrap of eternity on this earth After that she would take the mound of risen dough roll it out with her hands dip little discs of it in boiling oil and then top them with tomato parmesan basil and oil Or she would roll the dough out into a big circle on a baking sheet add basil tomato oil and mozzarella and bake it for twenty minutes in the hot oven

In the evenings we would sit at the kitchen table overlooking this sea finite flayed furrowed by ships carrying centuries gold millennia wines spices oils handicrafts freemen slaves This sea struck by waves by lights which never forgets a vessel a lighthouse a house This sea of buried dead And back come the millennia and centuries past the buried and reanimated dead and dark women hunched shrunken They weave cloth by the sea They wait rip stitch add rip hook gather They give substance to the sea A sea written drawn corporeal They make it the open closed body of the age-old sea barred with columns with vessels with lighthouses Sea of war sea of earth paper sea of flesh paper Egyptian Sicilian African sea Italian sea Sea of Spain France Greece Albania Roman sea inked hand-crafted articulated sea fatigued never tired of setting forth Mediterranean

We ate pizza and salad with broccoli tomato potatoes and green beans dressed in garlic basil oregano vinegar and oil drizzled over the fresh steamed vegetables We would eat in silence I hung on to my brother so as not to hear my father's gnashing teeth and crunching jaws as he ate wordlessly as if merely sitting with us was a concession to my mother At Christmas he didn't accept her gifts He would open the packages and put everything away until the next year when someone finally decided to use the socks or robe she had given him the year before Every Christmas our mother would become sad and cry at this form of rejection and disregard for her attention and care but my father too was tired worn down by his job selling fabric all over Campania and Lazio One day he brought home a Jewish textile merchant named Ettore Diveroli who'd sold out his stock of fabrics Our mother wasn't comfortable with my father's associates but she drew on her age-old culinary wisdom for them all the same Knowledge of food was knowledge of the Mediterranean centuries that lived on in my mother's eyes She prepared a meal worthy of a New Year's feast for Diveroli and our father She made tagliatelle with clams and sole in butter and poached salmon That morning she took me aside and showed me how She kneaded flour eggs water salt and a drop of oil into a dense stretchy dough Then she rolled it out on the counter She left the thin rings of pasta to rest on the flour and then rolled them up and cut them into thin strips In the evening she boiled the pasta and dressed it with oil and all the fish The Jewish merchant complimented her and greedily devoured her wise foods My mother looked on barely eating at all When she cooked a lot and was tired she would reject her own wisdom Her ancient sadness infected me Therein derived the germ of sin and excess I later saw in food First it was something divine simple and natural and later became something controlled regimented and overwhelming But food conserves the nature of the ages and the wisdom of God That was when I stripped away my childhood which perhaps I'd already buried when my grandmother died and I became what I was: a being destined just as my mother was to pass on the wisdom of the ages in food Our food contains all the knowledge that lives in this sea finite flayed furrowed by ships carrying centuries gold millennia wines spices oils handicrafts freemen slaves This sea struck by waves by lights which never forgets a vessel a lighthouse a house This sea of buried dead And back come the millennia and centuries past the buried and reanimated dead and dark women hunched shrunken They weave cloth by the sea They wait rip stitch add rip pierce gather They give substance to the sea A sea written drawn corporeal They make it the open closed body of the age-old sea barred with columns with vessels with lighthouses Sea of war sea of earth paper sea of flesh paper Egyptian Sicilian African sea Italian sea Sea of Spain France Greece Albania Roman sea inked handcrafted articulated sea fatigued never tired of setting forth Mediterranean

Sitting at the neighbor's table we ate the escarole pie that you make by rolling out dough on a baking sheet and stuffing it with bitter escarole wilted and tossed with sugar salt pine nuts olives and raisins I contained the wisdom of the ages The neighbor enjoyed its fruits but like my daughter couldn't cook and showed disinterest My daughter was eighteen and wanted to move out and leave town She never went to the neighbor's shoe shop The neighbor's talent was cleaning the way mine was cooking Every day she carefully dusted the house and the store the register the shelves the shoes and the windows Hungry and gluttonous after her husband's death food was nearly the only thing she enjoyed The blue-and-white store sparkled clean Everyone gawked at the woman baring her mature blond arms Irrepressible curls escaped from her bun Aging's no picnic in the sticks Men don't even look at you and women badmouth your independence and your past pleased to see your youthful graces fade This was the oppression my daughter wanted to escape To distract her I started thinking about a trip to the sea for us three lone women That night at dinner I said let's take the train to a beach town I know from my youth I was thinking of Torca a spot in Sant'Agata sui Due Golfi where you can see the Dolphin and the other two Galli islands where Nureyev and Lorca Massine had homes and where a childhood friend died jumping off a rock When we were young and went to the house in Torca we'd roast a tray of potatoes onions and tomatoes with oil It was simple good food Making good use of simple ingredients simple flavors is part of age-old Mediterranean wisdom

The landscape of streams canals creeks irrigating the rice fields and the poplars extending in regular rows between the dams and the Martesana At the house in Torca surrounded by stars and delicate baby's breath we would gaze out at the mist and the constellations all the stars and icosahedra in the sky

At the table here we gazed out at the landscape of fog and crime where in winter conflict incest and crime exploded along the Martesana in a landscape imbued with Leonardesque sorrow The fog of the Po Lowlands inspired infinite ennui And all that ennui took my mind back to our trip to the sea and I recalled Turchillo our dog in Torca darting between our legs like a little devil Then I looked back out at the fog waiting for the women to speak

Thinking about that trip it occurred to me that our children are other to us Once they're grown we see them as individuals with their own lives The total attachment that binds baby to mother is gone The placental detachment a mother may dread for so long finally happens It's less painful to see them leave us behind and walk tall down their own path toward their own destiny You stop wondering what their lives will become and whether they'll get married and have children or go off to live in London New York Paris You proceed down parallel yet communicating paths That takes my mind to friends and how all our work is talent endowed with its own force Sitting in the kitchen it was less painful to see my daughter's disinterest in the house and the age-old art of cooking We all choose our own life I didn't need her to resemble me She was other than me My mind drifted back to Torca and the days I spent there with friends at Christmastime when it was cold and the olive trees shimmered metallic in the pale sun and we went out to have fun hang out have sex I remembered Marina with her Botticellian face smiling at me from an immeasurable distance My first unfulfilled love She was like a father standing in for the patriarchal realm which I had yet to enter My daughter had and that's perhaps why she took no interest in the feminine arts of cooking and housekeeping I was revisiting my past I went back to the Tricarico Hotel which extended room after room in a concatenation of corridors that my grandfather managed and guarded I recalled the little checked dress my mother made me when I was a girl All my clothes were the product of her magisterial will of her seamstress's hands that contained the Mediterranean wisdom of textiles and sewing The same knowledge that inspired the fishermen of Positano when the number of fish diminished and they couldn't support themselves to turn to hand-dyeing and sewing beautiful rough fabrics Together with their wives they tinted them and made simple dresses and bathing costumes that made a bright backdrop in Nietzschean colors in that pearl of the Mediterranean Now that ancient knowledge has disappeared replaced by the beige taupe black and white of designer brands Among the olive trees and lemon groves and orange gardens color once gleamed against the great ramparts of the sky

The next day I made pizzaiola which is done by pan-cooking chicken or veal cutlets with fresh tomatoes oil basil garlic and salt I also made pork liver wrapped in caul fat with bay leaf and thick slices of Venetian veal liver cooked with onion slivers and dressed with oil a little butter sugar salt and a splash of milk and then vegetables agrodolce: zucchini eggplant carrot and scallion sautéed in oil sugar vinegar and salt

The gluttonous neighbor in her florid middle-agedness ate everything under the disapproving eye of my daughter who felt extraneous in that provincial context of lonely women She saw her mother's kitchen as the effect of a castration and a renunciation of better things She would probably leave I didn't know with whom or for where or how she'd get by but it no longer tormented me I saw men and women all over the Po Lowlands put one foot in front of the other and kilometers and insects and lightbulbs while algae flowed in the canals like long green hair They lived by the clock buying butter cookware TVs dinosaurs insects and lightbulbs Children put one foot in front of the other going to school to lunch to learn to live meanwhile the planet increased in missiles aims plans nuclear reactors waiting to hit the edge of the abyss But all this didn't torment me anymore

I let life flow by and into the distance without leaving anything behind without waste without regrets without pain Without anger at death I'm less afraid I've done what I could— Lord—give me the peace I've earned I've worked I've been a mother I didn't do all the good I could have I didn't go off to be a missionary like I wanted when I was young I didn't waste my talents but I didn't love myself Now in the kitchen I feel the grip of my chains slacken

One night I brought struffoli to the neighbor's: the simple Neapolitan Christmas treat made of honey and fried dough covered with sprinkles The austere and ancient sweetness of Greek cheese honey and dough from the rugged ancient land of the Peloponnesus and the tang of tragedy Our struffoli and our cathedrals of sweets and pastry and pasta preserve the pomp of the seventeenth and eighteenth centuries in Naples when

Volaire and Germans and Flemings came to paint Vesuvius which they depicted erupting red with fire and fervor in its age-old rock tufa lava shell bursting from its internal fiery torment Our pizza contains Pulcinella and Queen Margherita and the ancient mother goddesses and the steatopygous black Madonnas symbols of a fertility divided between the opulence of extreme rotundity and the austerity of the korai And our communion host and our mostaccioli cookies for Christmas and the dead hold the rituals of the Etruscans mixed with those of the Romans and Oscans when this was the home of Isis and Osiris

Our bread with tomato salt and oil and our pork sausage contain the orgies of the royalist masses and the madness of Masaniello and the gallows on which the Austrians and the Bourbons hanged Eleonora Fonseca Pimentel and Gennaro Serra di Cassano

Our refined pastiera preserves the pomp of the courts The humble one harks back to a people still tied to their Oscan and Greek past For the rich pastiera you roll out buttery pastry dough on a baking dish You fill it with ricotta mixed with melted sugar wheat berries candied fruit dark chocolate flakes and orange blossom water You criss-cross the top with thin strips of dough and bake it until it turns golden brown The poor pastiera is made of simple pastry filled with ricotta sugar and candied fruit The poor use lard for flavor The rich bring pastiera to its full splendor during Easter by adding almond paste and multicolored Jordan almonds The glorious people murderous and vile are appeased with this rustic recipe from Magna Graecia

I shared these stories and sentiments about food with the neighbor and my daughter It was late We were tired We went to sleep I thought I would buy the tickets for the trip to the sea tomorrow I'd book a pensione It's hard to look back at the past years later Perhaps I would never return to the mythical house in Torca I didn't know yet I drifted into the hollow groove of sleep

The next day I went to the kitchen and made the neighbor pumpkin pasta by sautéing the squash in oil with garlic and parsley and adding it to spaghetti al dente The colors of Van Gogh exploded in the orange and green Then I stopped by the station in the Po Lowlands filled with fog and crime I wanted to buy the tickets for the Amalfi Coast I hesitated It's hard to revisit the past The landscape with rows of poplars and larches and rice fields was entrancing with its gray damp under the vault of the sky and it made me long for this sea finite flayed furrowed by ships carrying centuries gold millennia wines spices oils handicrafts freemen slaves This sea struck by waves by lights which never forgets a vessel a lighthouse a house This sea of buried dead And back come the millennia and centuries past the buried and reanimated dead and dark women hunched shrunken They weave cloth by the sea They wait rip stitch add rip hook gather They give substance to the sea A sea written drawn corporeal They make it the open closed body of the age-old sea barred with columns with vessels with lighthouses Sea of war sea of earth paper sea of flesh paper Egyptian Sicilian African sea Italian sea Sea of Spain France Greece Albania Roman sea inked handcrafted articulated sea fatigued never tired of setting forth Mediterranean

I roamed the halls which were cold and silent at that hour and the stacks of scrapped tracks and retired cars covered in lichen and ivy and rubble as the international trains headed for distant destinations zipped past I went back home where my daughter told me she wanted to go to France by herself I said "Stay" She gave me one of those endless smiles that engulf

their recipient and replied "I have to go" That night I made
her Sicilian cassata I was using the ancient wisdom of food
to chain a creature who I had just realized was other than me
I crushed toasted green pistachios and almonds with sugar On
a tray I placed sponge cake made of sugar flour egg yolks and
whipped egg whites I added ricotta mixed with melted sugar
candied fruit dark chocolate flakes and more ricotta I flipped
it and covered the cassata with candied flowers and leaves It
was the apotheosis of color Cassata preserves the pomp of
the European courts that met at the royal palace facing Piazza
Plebiscito whose back bore the solemn weight of kings The
Austrians the French the Normans the Bourbons and Charles
of France and Frederick of Swabia It is a glorious dessert the
richest and most sumptuous from the Kingdom of the Two
Sicilies My daughter eyed it suspiciously She sensed that
I wanted to hold her back In the youth of our lives—Reader—
reflected in the primordial soup and the icosahedra of the
sky—we set sail on a ship that bears our name alone It was a
sad and silent meal My daughter went to pack The next morning she left for the station by herself Her backpack had just
socks and underwear and a sweater and pajamas a scarf and
gloves She wanted to see Antibes Nice Picasso Matisse and
eat bouillabaisse made with seafood and rice and bread and
tomato and fish She crossed the Po Lowland landscape of fog
and crime She gazed out at the rice fields and rows of poppies
maples and birches into which she was born The breaking day
dissipated in the ennui that dwindled in the northern light
as day broke Moss and lichen crept up the tetragonal and
steatopygous art nouveau structures like Moretti's majestic hydroelectric power station in Trezzo sull'Adda and the
industrial complex in Crespi d'Adda built according to the
industrial paternalism of Owen and Fourier In the light that

streamed from the sky my daughter was a lunar creature She held the package of food I had given her From home I saw the train depart and I turned to the statues in the station in their stony sleep watching people head for unknown destinations Then I was gripped by melancholy as if her destination was death Every time she leaves I'm assailed by thoughts of death I wonder How will I bear not seeing her face for eternity?

Alone under the icosahedra of heaven and the flesh of God I shut myself in the kitchen That was the terrain of my eternity as it was for my mother I made a casatiello It was almost March, a cold March It was almost spring Birds mosquitoes flies darted through the air I took flour cracklings lard water and pepper and put the eggs to boil I mixed everything into a soft dense dough and placed it in a round tin with four boiled eggs at east north west and south the sign of the cross marked on their shells I baked it until it turned golden It was a simple peasant dish I took the casatiello to the neighbor's by myself We ate in silence My mind drifted back to Antibes and I recalled Matisse and Picasso and the Fauves and the Corniche d'Or Picasso watched over the little town My gluttonous neighbor bit into the casatiello which contains the knowledge of the peasant age I told her about my daughter leaving She looked at me with one of those smiles that engulf their recipients like gifts from the heavens Now I thought of my daughter as something of mine that had detached from me She had left She was going far away I couldn't follow My longing was infinite

The next day I made the neighbor pasta with broccoli to eat at the table by ourselves I made it by sautéing the broccoli in a pan with garlic and oil and mixed it with long pasta We sat at the table as the icosahedra of the heavens continued their celestial dance and the great ramparts of the earth towered over us like giants on night watch I kept thinking of my daughter and again my mind went to the gun in the drawer I wondered whether I would ever use it but I had the ancient art of cooking in my soul Perhaps that would save me I suggested to myself after the seaside trip going to stay at a sanitarium where I'd been before It was a villa in the Po Lowlands surrounded by the landscape of fog and crime that watched us through the window as we ate our pasta

The past weighed on me like never before The landscape of the Po Lowlands accentuated my sadness The poplars the birches the maples the oaks formed woven rows that ran by the thousand then a hundred then a thousand more like ships toward their destiny I thought of my daughter as a creature I had raised with every care Too much care—Reader—and it had pushed her away I had bound her with ties of love too tight for an only child without a father My husband died in a road accident that mutilated his legs Then he went into intensive care and into a coma I had them pull the plug The remorse that came from the uncertainty of whether I'd committed a crime led my mind to the gun I kept in a drawer in the kitchen where shamanically I practiced the ancient art of the age-old wisdom of food that belongs to this sea finite flayed furrowed by ships carrying centuries gold millennia wines spices oils handicrafts freemen slaves This sea struck by waves by lights which never forgets a vessel a lighthouse a house

I made the neighbor rice with chickpeas I slow-cooked the beans without soaking them first and added rosemary garlic and oil Then I mixed them with rice and mixed pasta: maccheroni tagliatelle ziti the way this simple peasant dish is always made I also prepared fagioli della regina by cooking borlotti beans in tomato sauce basil and garlic with rice and mixed pasta These are simple Neapolitan dishes In the kitchen the noble Neapolitan people makes no distinction between high and low rich and humble or simple Neither the rich nor the courtiers or entrepreneurs or petite bourgeoisie or merchant class disdained putting beans on their table To distract me from nostalgia my mind wandered to the Neapolitan nativity scenes I had seen years before with my daughter and husband The porcelain statuettes were dressed in fine cotton silk satin and lace Their limbs were slender like heavenly creatures At the Certosa di San Martino where the nativity scenes were my daughter wanted to get a red coral and gold cornicello She too loved beautiful and gratuitous things that radiate the absolute light of things that exist whether we see them or not

In silence the neighbor and I also ate the stuffed chicken I prepared by deboning a whole bird and sewing it back up with thread filled with cubes of prosciutto and old bread soaked in milk and mixed with salt parmesan ricotta basil and sausage bits

This total devotion to food was getting me as fat as one of Botero's big women and my mind drifted to the gun Then I had the idea of making my house into an elegant and exclusive trattoria in the Po Lowlands amid the rice fields the streams the fog the crime With the restaurant I would provide for mouths other than my own I didn't want to become a being ruled by hunger I told the neighbor I was going to turn my sitting room into an elegant and exclusive dining space with little lamps and flowers on the tables covered with embroidered linens my mother had left me I would find suppliers through the wealthy butcher I'd met at the sanitarium last year who made roulades and meatballs and rotisserie chickens for the whole town

Before throwing myself into such an endeavor I wanted to give myself a little rest at the Villa Maria Luigia in Monticelli outside of Parma its grounds surrounded by poplars oaks and acorns against the landscape of fog and crime against a lunar backdrop I looked out from the neighbor's kitchen at the icosahedra in the sky dancing in the primordial soup from which all life forms come

The next day my daughter got back from France The week had crept by I went to pick her up at the station Under the stone statues I saw a sea of people My heart pounded like I was waiting for a lover I scanned the steel and stone above and below with increasing hope The restaurant plan distracted me from the gun I wasn't so apprehensive or possessive The train braked with a screech of metal bolts rails and wheels Out came a woman I barely recognized In seven days she'd become a woman I asked her what did you do? She just replied that she had seen Antibes Picasso the Corniche d'Or and Nice and had eaten pâté and bouillabaisse France had taken ahold of her heart She just said "I'm moving there" "Did you meet a man Did you fall in love?" Yes she had met a young engineer who worked at a marine pleasure craft company "I'm going to visit him as much as I can" she said simple and direct Her distant future no longer terrified me I saw men and women in the Po Lowlands put one foot in front of the other buying butter cookware insects dinosaurs lightbulbs TVs None of it tormented me anymore I watched the algae flowing in the canals like long green hair grazing the walls of my future Neapolitan restaurant I already saw it silhouetted against the landscape of fog and crime with a discreet little neon sign I asked my daughter to tell me about him She just said that he was separated and had a young daughter My daughter wanted to study and to go to France with her new love Like me she loved books more than anything Our house was filled with art books history science philosophy and literature I told her about my plan She enthusiastically approved We were two free women alike and equal in our life plans Now we loved each other without chains or restrictions Back at home I served her the casatiello I had saved She ate it without reserve without regrets without resentment without leaving anything behind She told me I'd need to find an assistant a cook an accountant and a server I told her I would defer those expenses until I turned a profit It was nice to look each other in the eye without possessiveness without darkness without waste without resentment without regret

It was late We watched the stars in the sky that endured in the music of chaos in the mad and mute music of the ico- sahedra of the sky The madness of existence in the geometry of chaos that exists for itself and for everyone swept us away on a lunar path of stars and comets I put her to bed tucking her in like she was a little girl whispering a few words about our future trip She was tired She murmured something and dropped her young head on the pillow I cooked and we ate together for another week in which I drew up plans and worked out figures for my future restaurant

Then she along with the neighbor were the ones taking me to the station I went to the sanitarium in Monticelli for a week where I could unburden myself of the daily housekeeping and cooking We got up at six in the morning and had breakfast with caffè d'orzo and cookies and toast and jam At noon and at six they brought us a first course of pasta and a second of meat or cheese or fish with a vegetable side At ten they gave us chamomile tea with sugar which sweetly ushered us into the night We strolled through the small dewy courtyard with its dry fountain Our feet sank into the acorns the leaves and the pine needles with a quick soft crunch You could see—Reader— unquiet souls in solitude in peace silently strolling the trails of desire smoking cigarettes The morning was spent chatting walking and doing crafts in the community room with Laura and Bruno drinking caffè d'orzo from a machine These are the sacred and austere places where the wounds of the soul are healed by taking a little break from life in the outside world You feel protected and provided for like when you were a child home sick and your mom would put a book an orangeade and a poached apple on your nightstand and a simple cutlet with warm broth A soft sun filters through the window shutters and we give in to the slow hours and the care of others without plans or even thoughts or concerns for the future Food prepared by others tastes of the gratuitous and the gift It's nice to be served sometimes in life

I decided I would lead the cooking group and pass on my ancient culinary knowledge to the others That way I made strides toward my future restaurant by guiding people in the kitchen I felt unburdened of the weight of my soul Even the past weighed on me less I thought less nostalgically of Torca of my friends from the past on the Amalfi Coast

I had the nurses and other patients make a Caprese cake which is done by mixing toasted ground almonds flour butter sugar melted dark chocolate rum espresso and whipped egg whites and baking the batter in a pan for half an hour until it becomes a dense cake that tastes strong and heavy and light at the same time It tastes of the sea and olive trees and almond blossoms and evenings spent drinking wine with friends by the sea and with the history that accompanies any food The Caprese is dark like the complexion of an Ethiopian or Saracen soldier

I talked to my daughter about her Frenchman She told me she'd met him one night when she was sad and walking alone down the shore in Antibes Her eyes were still full of Matisse's *La Danse* Provence in its splendor had swept her up in a dream of never-ending youth and she felt the power of chaos alive inside her like hot magma Everything in her young and inexpert heart was waiting to burst She'd stepped into a café and asked for a light wine She drank in a daze like Degas's absinthe drinker and a young man came up to her He took her hand without speaking and she let herself be chained by that direct and uninhibited gaze that seemed to come from an infinite distance It was a gaze that contained all the knowledge of the ages She gave this man one of those smiles that engulf their recipient like rivers cascading from the springs of chaos which contain the primordial fetus that hovered over the houses of Antibes He had rescued her from her melancholy by passing on to her the dark and luminous knowledge in his eyes that showed the way to his heart

I watched her as she talked and I saw in her the woman she was Full of expectations of fears of fury of anger of calm of torment all embedded in her life like scarlet marks of the hopes in my own soul Now she was opening her soul to me and showing me the wounds and holes and seams Like me she had a spine of iron and dead children's bones Sitting at the table in the kitchen we ordered the bones of creation as well as our souls Way up high the bones mixed in with the icosahedra of the sky with the stardust in the way up high of the world They were the bones of the primordial fetus that lives in every creature and thing In the closets we put the phalanges of the hands that have worked so hard In the drawers the tarsals the metatarsals of the feet that have walked so far and the tibias and the fibulas of the legs that have traveled so long down the endless and mysterious roads of the earth And in every cavern of dust and on every cushion we stowed the bones of our aching souls that now flooded the surrounding world with the smiles of a mother and a daughter joined in commonality and peace I didn't think of the gun Then I gave her a recipe and together we went to make brioche just like my mother did with her ancient culinary wisdom You mix flour eggs sugar milk butter and yeast You work the batter in a big bowl and smack it raising your arm high over the golden wheat The dough leavens and swells like an erupting volcano With the vehemence and violence released you leave it to rest for an hour Then bake the product of this joyous battle in a hot oven for half an hour and you have a little mound of gold and stardust and golden wheat like a plow-furrowed field

We ate it together with the neighbor My daughter didn't disdain the ancient art of cooking She talked some more about France and I showed her my plan for the future restaurant In the sitting room with the four big windows overlooking the garden I would put six round tables I would leave the book-shelves and the desk where I sat to read and write in my journal where that day I wrote "My daughter gave me a heavenly smile full of sky" This sentence contained the sense of an entire life and of two lives spent in the fray of the radiant and tenebrous love that binds a mother and a daughter In my journal I kept this poem

> *woman, don't worry*
> *don't think of the shape*
> *things take*
> *take your child*
> *your day with your work*
> *for them*
> *your child will have children*
> *and their children's children*
> *and their children*
> *so what if the neighbor broke*
> *your glass*
> *today it's you too and you and you*
> *and you and you and you*

It was a notebook of handmade paper from Amalfi in pale cerulean blue like the color of the sky and the river in the early morning when the sun hides on the opposite side of creation while the deciduous queens of heaven form a chorus for the primordial fetus that lives in the eternal magma of chaos

I was happy to have a new life plan With the ancient knowledge contained in my hands open to this sea finite flayed furrowed by ships carrying centuries gold millennia wines spices oils handicrafts freemen slaves This sea struck by waves by lights which never forgets a vessel a lighthouse a house

I started making figurines out of salt dough I mixed equal parts water flour and extra fine salt with a drop of oil and I wove garlands of flowers and shoots and vines and little dolls with long dresses and wide hats I made spheres and studded them with pebbles and shells I baked everything in the oven and painted them pastel colors I used them as decorations for the tables Some I gave away to my first customers from the neighborhood who having learned of my intentions had already asked if they could come for dinner The old butcher and his wife were there The wealthiest entrepreneurs in the area I was happy to make objects and foods for mouths other than my own and my neighbor's I proudly showed my daughter the fruits of my effort and as a token of affection I gave her a cobalt-blue ornament covered with waves and shells

The next day I made a pasta casserole so everything would be ready in case anyone came for dinner In a baking dish I put pasta and béchamel made with butter salt flour and milk I added a layer of breadcrumbs and then cubes of prosciutto tomato sauce little meatballs peas and mozzarella I was starting to earn money for myself for the first time since teaching My life was filling up with joy

I found myself in the harmony of the celestial spheres in the chaos that orders the bones of creation every day and night in the creation that dances in the primordial soup that contains the divine fetus that orders the bones of the demons and angels of Anubis and Lethe and Demeter and Persephone and Astaroth and Christ and Buddha and Mohammed and Allah and the twelve apostles and the saints and the hanged the blessed the damned the drowned and the saved of creation The order of chaos is contained in the celestial spheres that rotate in every direction and in the compass rose and in the infernal rocks overlooking the abyss at the core of this place we call earth contained in this sea finite flayed furrowed by ships carrying centuries gold millennia wines spices oils handicrafts freemen slaves This sea struck by waves by lights which never forgets a vessel a lighthouse a house This sea of buried dead And back come the millennia and centuries past the buried and reanimated dead and dark women hunched shrunken They weave cloth by the sea They wait rip stitch add rip hook gather They give substance to the sea A sea written drawn corporeal They make it the open closed body of the age-old sea barred with columns with vessels with lighthouses Sea of war sea of earth paper sea of flesh paper Egyptian Sicilian African sea Italian sea Sea of Spain France Greece Albania Roman sea inked handcrafted articulated sea fatigued never tired of setting forth Mediterranean

The order of creation that keeps the bones in order lives in the heart of all creatures It lives in your heart it lives in mine—Reader—it lives in the leaves the rocks the hills the streams the houses the factories the offices the industrial complexes that send their organic and radioactive waste into the winds contaminating the planet with the debris of a perennial war in a time of peace In the kitchen I wrote in my journal And you—Reader—do you have children? Do you keep a diary?

Keep it on your nightstand keep it in your bed take it on the road carry it in your house

I started mine at fifteen I wrote poems in it Now it lies abandoned among my dusty papers It seems banal to keep writing the same things

You're wrong—Reader—a journal preserves the remains of everything we've done that we've said that we've dreamed What we've wanted what we've had what we've shared What we've left behind What you've said to me what I've said to you what I've done to you what you've done to me What we've gone through what we've seen The languages we've known the people who've loved us the ones who've hated us the ones who thought we were nobody the ones who were nobody to us What we've felt what we've eaten what we've generated what we've thought what we've been told what we've followed What we've believed what we have navigated written counted Everything we've traversed What has penetrated us what hasn't even touched us That God we've believed in those angels those dreams those myths those washing machines those detergents those comic books those memories those children those groceries those potatoes those medicines those cuts those stitches those wounds we've received and those we've given What we've pretended not to see and what we didn't want to hear What we've sung sewn combed washed fixed That newspaper that book that window that view those churches those houses those hospitals these roads the entire road we've taken What we're born as what we die as What we've left kissed struck What has kissed us what has burned us That hair those shoes those closets those streets those colors those planes those buildings we've visited those crimes we've perpetrated What we haven't done said dreamed What we could have what we wished we had what we didn't put out what we didn't leave eat feel what we didn't even want What we were not born as what we did not die as What I didn't tell you what you didn't tell me what I didn't see in you what I didn't say to you Everything we didn't go through what we didn't read defeat love what we didn't follow what didn't kiss us what didn't burn us What we didn't say to each other what we didn't share The hand we didn't give the laundry we didn't hang the closets we didn't open those crimes we didn't see those faces those voices that world we didn't know those stars we dreamed of What I wanted to give to you do to you eat you vomit you What we are not what we won't be what we never were What they'll leave with us when we no longer see hear feel What the earth will know of us hitting us clump by clump under the flowers under the plaque in the middle of all the other flowers other plaques other stones other graves other dead

Now I write—Reader—in my journal that I'm happy I'm becoming a businesswoman Without any advertising people from all around are starting to come to my restaurant I'm making woven bracelets necklaces and frames and figurines out of salt dough and painting bases with acrylic and tempera I mix equal parts flour extra fine salt and a spoonful of oil and water Then I put the molds in the oven to bake The customers are elated by these products of ancient knowledge from the hands of a fifty-year-old single mother Manual wisdom is a gift from God a conquest obtained by work and passed down in our double-helix DNA for generations by the thousand and a thousand more beyond The past is the giants on the pillars of our shoulders Let us carry them—Reader—as a light and sacred load

Bring your past—Reader—into your life Bring your dirty and learned hands Remember you can't get dirty if you're dead When you die the bones of creation and your soul must be put in order Dirty your life—Reader—mix it with gray matter and snot and blood and oil and muck and tempera and pen and food and feces and the colors of the sky of nostalgia of peace of war of battle make it climb the steps of the sky up to the icosahedra of chaos that sing in the celestial spheres and in the primordial soup that contains the divine fetus in which you can see—Reader—ships and more ships sailing by the thousand then a hundred then another thousand on the surface of the seas let God ask you

"Are you dead, Reader?"

Go ahead and reply "I'm dead" In return you'll have a new life to climb the steps of the heavens full of iron and the bones of dead children and the living Ascend like a warrior weary of war and bloodshed Surrender to your death and your life—Reader—it's the only one you've been given Hold it dear spend it well treat it with every care Love yourself above all things and you will be able to love your God

After writing in my journal I got to work in the kitchen for the restaurant That evening I took some old potatoes and made them into a soft and crumbly dough They became a dense and compact mash I stirred the steamed potatoes with milk butter eggs salt parmesan and basil layered them on the buttered pan with breadcrumbs with layers of mozzarella and prosciutto and peas and basil and béchamel On top I poured béchamel made with flour butter milk salt and baked it for thirty minutes I had a dish ready to heat up on the spot for my patrons There were the postman the mayor the doctors from the hospital in Monticelli where I live in the landscape of fog and crime of the Po Lowlands There were doctors and nurses from the sanitarium where I'd stayed and where I wanted to return to alleviate the fatigue from my life of abundant and profitable production My hands never rest—Reader—And for that night with the help of my daughter and the neighbor I also prepared a roast goose stuffed with sausage chestnuts chicken lard and basil and bread mixed with parmesan and ricotta and a ragù I made sautéing onion carrot celery in oil and meat simmered with just a touch of tomato sauce for an hour

I also made a timbale by mixing lard and flour and salt to make a thin pastry crust which I filled with tagliatelle and little meatballs and sausage and peas dressed in a rich and succulent Genovese sauce made with carrot celery basil and ample tomato and meat I covered the timbale with the crust and put it in the oven for thirty minutes until it turned golden brown I prepared a pie and a stew with carrots potatoes peas and little bits and chunks of chicken and veal until it became a tender mix of meats For dessert I prepared struffoli the Neapolitan Christmas treat made by golden-frying little pieces of dough and covering them with sprinkles and candied fruit and candied violets I made a savory pie with shortcrust filled with artichokes potatoes peas and chunks of chicken I also made an Olivier salad by cutting and steaming chopped cabbage peas carrots and beets in a light and frothy mayonnaise made by blending egg yolk beaten whites lemon and oil I garnished the salad with the mayonnaise dressing along with cabbage olives pickles and anchovies A dish of age-old wisdom from Great Russia and the Mediterranean I looked out at the celestial spheres and the icosahedra of the sky dancing like the figures in Matisse's *La Danse* in Antibes

It was seven and the smells from my kitchen spread through the hungry and gluttonous town Everyone's mouths watered seeing my windows fogged up from cooking and steam They came in droves They squeezed around the tables It was a buffet of insatiability They ate that food obscenely salivating and crapulent It was the flesh of God Steam from the kitchen billowed into the dining room where I had set out my salt dough necklaces and figurines and bracelets and frames The corpulent opulent ladies snatched them up covetously They were made by the sweat of my hands Oh hands Hands— Reader—hands can be sold they can be bought Hands rape they abuse they live in themselves absorbing and radiating the energy they've used to make near nothing into the everything of human art and handicrafts that contain the honor of work well done and with passion To cook or to create you don't use your mind you use the art of observing the world and relishing it and harmonizing tastes smells colors to make a beautiful painting or a simple loaf of bread or a typewriter After years of school and thought my tired brain rested in my hands

Come eight the wine and beer ran in rivers The men lit up cigars between courses and sweating they loosened coats and vests Some came in from the street hungry and gluttonous The contagion of the great feast had spread to the entire street and the town The women brushed hair off sweaty brows We kept bringing wine and bread that disappeared into the bottomless bellies of the diners in the big room in the fat and opulent Po Lowlands The thought of our seaside trip was distant There was so much work I saw wealthy and modest Padan businessmen and fat bourgeois sweating in their obscene swollen clothes Steam from the gateaux and the casserole and the goose wafted into the firmament brightening and obscuring a night of indulgence By ten the room was covered in crumbs on the tablecloths and scraps on the ground Wine dotted the tablecloths given to me by my mother who had taught me the ancient Mediterranean knowledge of cooking When the roast goose arrived it was met with expressions of ecstasy The commensals helped themselves from serving dishes excising slices of meat they gulped down with bread and wine No one around those parts had ever seen a goose so big and fat Their bellies and heads were stuffed with food

My daughter and the neighbor and I hid out in the kitchen as the great Padan feast dwindled down like a dying fire among the weary sweats and murmurs at the end of a colossal consumption

The success took so much out of me And I had doubts about the trip too The work took me away from a part of myself I decided that the next evening I wouldn't open and I brought in an assistant cook The vapors dissipated in the dining room Meanwhile the fat bourgeois shuffled off into the landscape of fog and crime of the Po Lowlands We put the few leftovers in the fridge I saw them put one foot in front of the other as algae swayed in the canals like long green hair under the ramparts of the sky It was one in the morning and silly with exhaustion we watched the deciduous queens of heaven dance and dance in the icosahedra of the sky I drank and fell into a rediscovered intoxication that dispelled all thought and care for the future There with my daughter and neighbor I stared at my hands in my lap Oh hands Hands—Reader—hands are sold washed they hug they bake they cook Hands think—Reader—They contain the knowledge of the centuries and millennia

Tired we went to bed The next morning at breakfast my daughter told me about her French future She wanted to teach in Antibes and start a family with her Frenchman Her life away from me didn't upset me anymore I would become a traveling grandmother I looked at her serene and once again I thought about the trip to the sea away from all worry But there was so much work it wasn't quite the time for a getaway The trip loomed ahead like a bright beacon against the background of our long teary and golden road

I pictured my daughter in her house in Provence with red-checked armchairs and dishes from Aix-en-Provence I could learn French cooking She gave me a questioning look I told her in France many years ago I'd seen a house with red-checked chairs and curtains and cushions and white-paneled windows and wood floors with a fireplace in the living room the whole place filled with ceramics from Aix-en-Provence a beautiful town on the hills of the Corniche d'Or full of tourists and sculptures by Miró

She told me about her Frenchman who had left his wife out of boredom He had a daughter he only saw once a week She was entrusted to her mother who looked after her with the utmost care She was a modest French teacher without pretensions The man was endowed with imagination and entrepreneurial spirit He wanted to open his own shipyard on the Côte d'Azur He had vision He liked traveling sailing swimming going to the cinema My daughter's determination at such a young age frightened me but in this she was like me I had been a teacher too and at this point in my life I was opening a restaurant all on my own

Together we went to prepare an apple-pineapple cake which you make by arranging slices of fresh pineapple and slices of apple in a buttered pan On top you pour a soft and light batter of egg flour yeast and sugar You bake it for thirty minutes until the cake turns golden Then you flip it so the outlines of the caramelized slices of fruit glisten on top

Then for the next evening we prepared tuna and potatoes which you make by mixing boiled potatoes with mayonnaise and pureed tuna capers olives and parsley You shape the mixture into a fish garnished with cabbage parsley carrot slices celery and lemon

My daughter was happy to take part in this culinary activity She received from my hands the ancient knowledge of food that lives in this sea finite flayed furrowed by ships carrying centuries gold millennia wines spices oils handicrafts freemen slaves

That day in my journal I wrote "My daughter is becoming a woman We cut the umbilical cord together She's going off on her way and I on mine but separation doesn't scare us Deep down we're closer than ever"

We looked out at the icosahedra in the sky dancing in the voice of chaos that sings in the primordial soup that occupies the great ramparts of the world and the steps of creation which puts its bones in order day after day in the harmony of the celestial spheres

Sitting at the kitchen table we gazed out at the sky at the icosahedra that went by the thousands like ships of creation My daughter looked at me affectionately With the restaurant closed that night she and the neighbor and I had made ourselves a meat broth by filling a pot with water and a piece of ox a shank bone potato carrot celery onion zucchini and parsley without oil After simmering for an hour the fat rises to the surface You let it sit for an hour and then skim the fat off the top Then make tagliolini by mixing flour eggs water and salt You knead it into a soft and stretchy dough then leave it to rest for an hour Then you roll it out into a sheet over a flour-covered surface You roll it up and cut it in thin strips then leave them to rest and dry When you're ready to eat you dunk them in boiling water and serve them with the finished broth and fresh parmesan

We also made a light vegetable soup with potatoes celery onion carrot parsley spinach and asparagus and more carrots into a mix of vegetables floating in broth You can also blend it into a potage and add as much pastina as you like

For the next night when I would reopen the doors to the restaurant the only family-run trattoria in the area we prepared trays of cannelloni We wrapped the sheets of tagliolini dough into little bundles filled with ground meat cooked in tomato sauce with ricotta and mozzarella and parmesan and little meatballs and peas and béchamel and cubes of prosciutto Topped with oil basil béchamel and tomato we put them in the oven on medium heat until they turned golden I bought the meat from the butcher in Monticelli who also had the biggest grocery around We cut the same pasta dough into panels and made lasagne too

We kept the cannelloni and vegetable soup for ourselves We ate in silence The fat and opulent and gluttonous neighbor ate voraciously The night before she'd also given in to the end-less and indiscriminate feasting In her life as a woman alone without a husband and without children food was the only satisfaction that presented itself after workdays spent in the company of empty shoes She spoke to them Some replied in the mysterious language of things that exist only to be looked at The shoes were arranged on the towering ramparts of the sky and the great bastions of the world They climbed the steps of creation of things which are the same Things are things—Reader—They thingify in the chaos in which creation is created matter materializes nature naturalizes And God godifies

The shoes on the shelves were enigmatic and potent pres-ences like korai like vestals of the temple of nothingness The eternal night hovered over them They were hieratic and empty like virgins robbed of the fruit of their womb by the violence of invading armies like the Austrians French Normans Saracens who raped this sea finite flayed furrowed by ships carrying centuries gold millennia wines spices oils handicrafts freemen slaves This sea struck by waves by lights which never forgets a vessel a lighthouse a house This sea of buried dead And back come the millennia and centuries past the buried and reanimated dead and dark women hunched shrunken They weave cloth by the sea They wait rip stitch add rip hook gather They give substance to the sea A sea written drawn corporeal They make it the open closed body of the age-old sea barred with columns with vessels with lighthouses Sea of war sea of earth paper sea of flesh paper Egyptian Sicilian African sea Italian sea Sea of Spain France Greece Albania Roman sea inked handcrafted articulated sea fatigued never tired of setting forth Mediterranean

I recalled the narrow streets of Amalfi and the ladders from which its inhabitants once threw boiling oil on their enemies In those streets I saw the figure of a man in chains in a cathedral from great Tsarist Russia being tortured with boiling oil being poured down his throat An atrocious death I tried to imagine dying by torture and up rose the glorious figures of the poets who died for truth in Tehran in Baghdad in Vietnam in Dresden in Warsaw in Dublin in Paris in Naples and in the concentration camps in Katowice and Auschwitz Reality is bigger than us

I looked calmly at the carefully prepared dishes and as I went to get bread and wine wrote in my journal "I'm happy to earn my own bread I did what my mother told me She said get a job for yourself be independent from men"

Her life as a housewife had always borne the chains of male dependence No man—Reader—loves his wife when she becomes nothing but his wife and the mother of his children Daily cares in their routine and tedium destroy the fluttering of youth My mother told me how when she was young she'd go to the Amalfi Coast She stayed at a beautiful hotel in Amalfi where after a night of love she'd go bring her lover warm croissants that they ate on the sweaty love-mussed sheets She took pictures of the enigmatic stone women at Villa Cimbrone in

Ravello She looked out onto the infinite of this sea finite flayed furrowed by ships carrying centuries gold millennia wines spices oils handicrafts freemen slaves

The terrace hung over a sheer cliffside and she felt a sense of infinite vertigo as if her entire life was sunken in that sea She didn't want to become a woman with a dustrag eternally in her hand She was a free spirit She liked to run swim play She was beautiful and admired with her Norman beauty by the men and women in Bagnoli She was the youngest of four siblings and the darling of her father from whom she got her infinite blue eyes Over the years the restlessness of youth came to rest in the ancient wisdom of her hands that had inherited from her mother's the Mediterranean wisdom of food

The neighbor talked about her shoes which she treated like living creatures and companions She filled their hollows with her war-weary hands Sometimes she measured them Then tired of the solitude of empty shoes she thought about replacing them with flowers We were sorry because her store of vestal virgins was the nicest in town filled with shoes in which you can see the lack of the person who will fill them Shoes are gravestones evoking human absence amid the furor of the world But there was time She would keep selling shoes for a few months longer

She ate gluttonously Her pinguitude emanated from her misshapen body I recalled my mother monitoring my food That was the start of the dependency that had kept me in chains and now that they had been loosened I was able to open the restaurant

We drank wine in the warm kitchen Outside it was almost spring but the Po Lowlands were still in the grips of the damp and silent cold That landscape of fog and crime and rows of poplars maples and birches and rice growing in the marshes in the evenings sending their steam into the icosahedra of the sky We looked out at the fog and after dinner we went to cook a fat hen in salted water for the next day I added celery carrot onion potato and parsley In the meantime my daughter talked about her French future She pictured herself cycling round the curves of the Corniche d'Or to her teaching job at some remote village in the beautiful hills of Provence Children maybe just one She loved musical and feminine French French is like the soft murmur of words spoken into a lover's ear In a photo I kept of my mother at Villa Cimbrone you could see a majestic stone woman doubled in reflection in a marsh She carried her double like a stowaway like the thousands and thousands of ships of death and of life that sail free over the back of the seas That terrace seemed like the last bastion of the known world where the eternal voice of chaos sang

That day I wrote in my journal "Like my mother I'm enchanted by the beauty of things She passed down to me the ancient knowledge contained in her hands"

After the shoes the neighbor wanted to be a florist That night for dinner we had semolina made by heating fine semolina flour with milk and dressing it simply with butter and parmesan and some leftover tomato sauce from the night before She told us about how when she was little she would go to the fields with her mother and pick flowers She'd dawdle at the cornflowers the poppies and the wildflowers Her mother told her "don't pick anything they're all living creatures" She didn't understand she just let herself be enchanted by the beauty of things that let in the piercing light contained in the celestial spheres that hold the harmony of chaos that lives inside this sea finite flayed furrowed by ships carrying centuries gold millennia wines spices oils handicrafts freemen slaves

At midday they'd return home and her mother would make minestrone with chopped potato carrot zucchini celery spinach turnip greens and bitter broccoli rabe mixed with milk and rice and garnished with oil butter and grated parmesan whisked with melted ricotta and a meatloaf made with fine-ground fatty beef mixed with eggs peas béchamel prosciutto cheese and baked golden accentuated by the egg yolk brushed on top as she did with all savory pies and baked pastas Then a plate of peaches in syrup with cherries and pastry cream made by mixing butter sugar milk potato starch and egg always stirring in the same direction to keep the cream from curdling She kept the fresh wine-soaked peaches for herself She gave the girl a plate of blood oranges and blond oranges dressed with salt oil and vinegar Her mother had also inherited from her mother the ancient wisdom that every woman conserves in their divided heart as ambivalent creatures half free from chains and torments and half bound to count and order the bones of creation from the first day of creation to the last to climb the steps of the sky and the tall ramparts of the world Day and night women always order the bones of the soul and of creation of the living and the dead

In the morning making the bed they put in the linen drawers the bones of the loved and unloved ones who live in their house and the bones of their ancestors shown in photographs picturing seashores and beaches and houses and bridges and roads from eras past Then they order the bones of their past when they were free and unencumbered without the weight of a family Women are laden with unearned burdens Women are creditors to men and God Their debt will be repaid before the courts of history and by the demons and angels standing in the hall of justice At history's end no one can judge the women Women have been raped in wars in their homes and in

43

concentration camps At least there death was swift Worse and just as deadly is the stillicide that wears away a soul abandoned exclusively to managing and maintaining a home Women see to maintaining the houses and bones of creation the crying room the joy room the living room the Sodom and Gomorrah room the room of the hedonists of the gluttonous the envious the lascivious the rooms of the circles of hell the rooms of the children of the fathers and the mothers Women keep them up every day dust them off

They dust they sweep they observe and it's because of their keen eye that rooms don't die don't disappear into nothingness Creation wouldn't last without the care and maintenance of rooms which is left to women The spines of iron and dead children's bones and all the living and the dead in history would vanish completely without a woman's eye to keep them Women live in rooms of bone of human flesh and God's flesh In their closets they keep the vacuum that sends its fury into the deafening boom of the world and in the blue boom of thunder that blasts the bridges and roads of history It was the same infernal rumble as my neighbor's vacuum Like every woman she too deafened and tormented the neighborhood and all the Po Lowlands with her torture device The vacuum was her revenge and her ball and chain Every woman wants one and prays pater noster qui es in coelis forgive me my debts as I have also forgiven my debtors We are all debtors and creditors before the court of history in which you too came down to immolate your flesh and bones to save the bones of the world and of history from death I absolve you of your absolute power You absolve me of my feminine pride that binds me to the absolute exhausting and eternal enterprise of maintaining the bones of creation

As the neighbor remembered her mother her recipes and the flowers she was distracted from eating the potatoes and rice we made by mixing golden rice and pearl rice with milk butter parmesan and diced potato It was a warm and hearty dish that with the fog of the Po Lowlands weighing down the air outside my kitchen warmed the souls inside the solitary house silhouetted against the sky An isolated structure between woven rows of poplars maples birches and oaks under the tall sky of an opulent Northern Italy maker of its own destiny We ate breaded mozzarella and croquettes and rice balls typical fried finger foods from the wisdom of Neapolitan cuisine You take slices of old bread dipped in milk then beaten egg You place mozzarella between the two slices of bread You take the sandwich and dip it in egg flour and breadcrumbs then fry it in boiling oil until it turns golden brown Then you mix old boiled potatoes with milk butter egg and parmesan until you have a stiff and thick dough that you shape into ovals filled with egg prosciutto peas cheese and fresh or buffalo mozzarella You fry them on high heat after coating them in beaten egg and flour and breadcrumbs making sure they don't fall apart You also coat the rice balls in egg flour and breadcrumbs mixing the cooked golden rice with cheese and egg You make round and oval balls with the rice filled with ragù and peas or with prosciutto peas hard cheese and soft cheese and mozzarella You can make them red with tomato or white with parmesan and milk

The neighbor ate hungrily but less gluttonously perhaps consoled by the idea of the flowers that distracted her from the boundless solitude of the shoes which contain the silence of the centuries and the absence of humanity

At the table I wrote in my journal "I used to pick flowers when I was little too I ripped the silk off of corn cobs to make hair for my dolls I'm a woman I'm a woman—my God—I take care of the bones of the world I'm tired of the burden Give me a flower Give me a kiss—Reader—Give me a flower give me a kiss—my God—make me feel like a woman without chains again But I love the bones—Lord—I maintain the bones which are the architecture of joy the architecture of pain which provides the structure of the architecture of the world and of history in the roar of battle in the labor camps in the concentration camps in the hospitals in the prisons in the courts in the sewers where the rats devour the eyes of the dead and the living The bones shine with droplets and frost Every house building hospital sky earth water river land cemetery contains the ossuary of the sky of God composed of a shroud and a structure of smooth and candid bones"

I closed the journal We went to bed My daughter kept talking about her future in France Without realizing it she was becoming a woman She was loading herself with bones to order: the bones of her students her child the French her husband her house on the Corniche d'Or We slept a deep sleep

The next morning I prepared for the evening when I'd reopen the restaurant for my patrons I made breaded mozzarella and croquettes and golden rice balls and fried lamb brain with vegetables made by coating in flour and beaten egg some potato cabbage zucchini onion eggplant and artichoke I fried everything on high heat then set it on metal trays to reheat before serving For dessert besides the Caprese cake I made custard cups by mixing milk flour sugar in a saucepan once cooled mixed with beaten egg whites I poured the mixture into a buttered pan and baked it in a bain-marie at medium heat I also made sweet ricotta cups with coffee powder cocoa and rum put them on little plates and garnished them with fresh fruit I also made little vegetable frittatas mixing egg with vegetables and parmesan salt and Roman ricotta: the vegetables were spinach rapini zucchini potatoes onion basil and rose and chard and broccoli rabe First I cooked lentils for half an hour with fresh tomato basil and garlic and a splash of milk which right before serving I would mix with pasta al dente and rice and then a big pot of clams and cockles steamed with garlic oil and parsley along with boned fresh anchovies With this dish that exudes saltiness and the scent of the Mediterranean paired with al dente spaghetti dressed in Cirio tomato passata Cirio the glorious Neapolitan preserves company I would bring warmth to my commensals' dinner My hands contained the ancient knowledge of food of women who see to the maintenance of the bones of creation through cooking On the ramparts of death and life I ordered the bones which have contained the harmony of the celestial spheres of history from the first day of creation to the last

2

That night with the knowledge of food passed down to me by my mother who like all women had spent her life setting the bones of a family at risk of breaking apart at every step because of the bad feelings and resentments between her and my father while all the time with her rag and duster she devoted herself to managing the architecture of pain of a house that stood on one of the most beautiful hills in Naples—with that ancient knowledge I prepared for my restaurant's next opening that night

As I cooked I recalled the hills above Via Tasso where we lived when we were little and I saw the towering and sacred figure of my mother putting flowers by the photographs of her dead and hanging the laundry out to dry with Assunta All women, my God, order the bones of creation with you to support buildings churches houses and bridges and roads and constellations and galaxies and planets and Milky Ways and meteorites and new worlds being formed where the voice of chaos sings where the harmony of the celestial spheres coheres

I made a lasagne casserole and two big trays of Olivier salad First I made the clam sauce for the spaghetti Then I put a big pot on the stove with tomato sauce in which I poured some scorpionfish squids clams octopus small codfish and mullet and wedge clams and cockles and calamari and shrimp along with fresh garlic and parsley to make a thick and succulent fish soup that contains all the ancient flavor of this sea finite flayed furrowed by ships carrying centuries gold millennia wines spices oils handicrafts freemen slaves This sea struck by waves by lights which never forgets a vessel a lighthouse a house This sea of buried dead And back come the millennia and centuries past the buried and reanimated dead and dark women hunched shrunken They weave cloth by the sea They wait rip stitch add rip hook gather They give substance to the sea A sea written drawn corporeal They make it the open closed body of the age-old sea barred with columns with vessels with lighthouses Sea of war sea of earth paper sea of flesh paper Egyptian Sicilian African sea Italian sea Sea of Spain France Greece Albania Roman sea inked handcrafted articulated sea fatigued never tired of setting forth Mediterranean

That night was misty and foggy with secrets and crimes and hideaways The entire neighborhood and town of Monticelli where I had lived for years after the death of my husband with whom I'd lived in Milan were abuzz Through the foggy air wafted the scent and labored-over flavor of a second great feast

I didn't know why my cooking awakened such base and bestial gluttonous urges It wasn't my intention when I cooked Perhaps it was the opulent southern air contained in my dishes which drove everyone to total satisfaction of desire which taken to extremes became its opposite Last time I'd seen some women and their companions get sick and go vomit in the bathrooms which I had to clean afterward I put these thoughts aside as I finished my plates with care

I gave the fish and tomato sauce a stir I brought bread and wine to the tables With the help of my daughter and neighbor who now always spoke of her flowers and her mother I decorated them with the little salt dough figurines and put others for sale in a big basket on the mantel I placed some logs and twigs in the fireplace that I kept going from the afternoon on It was still cold even though it was almost spring And as we worked I told my daughter about the Milan years with her father

I came to the North on a cold winter day accompanied by Santa and Alfredo two dear old friends Before me beckoned a future full of hopes as happens with all young women who go to join a man they love in a distant place For me a woman of the South the foggy and silent North of frost and ice held a certain appeal I was glad to hold in my memory's bones the glorious image of the sublime Neapolitan landscape and reduce it in my heart to the flatness of the Lombard plains which extended as far as the eye could see once the car passed the Romagna border and we saw the steam rising skyward from the rivers and canals That Leonardesque landscape was full of anticipation I pictured myself biking to a neighborhood on the outskirts of town or taking the train to the suburbs to teach When we arrived in Milan we met my future husband at Italimpianti where he worked as an engineer

Santa and Alfredo left the next day and my solitary life began Every day he went to work I had a teaching position but it was still temporary I didn't get a call right away So that was when I first began to use the ancient knowledge of food and handicrafts that my mother had passed down to me I made delicious suppers for the two of us and little objects out of salt dough and terracotta that I tried to sell in the shops by my house At night when he came home we would eat go to the cinema and make love They were beautiful glorious years We got married in a simple ceremony at city hall We decorated the house with cheap furniture bought at Trivulzio or the outdoor markets We were happy with these little things

For that night I also made roast beef and pork loin by oven roasting the shank with thyme and bay and in a big casserole a string-tied tender cut of ox I quick-braised it in wine to keep it

50

rare The pork was also quick I made some Milanese veal cutlets coating double-cut chops in flour egg and breadcrumbs and as a side I prepared a tray of roasted potatoes with rosemary and oil and salt and some light and fluffy potato-carrot puree I prepared a mix of tastes and smells and colors Lombard and Neapolitan The aroma of the roasts wafted through the foggy kitchen windows The neighborhood was frenzied and obsessed I didn't know what was going to happen that evening and as I was cooking and talking with my daughter about her father and us and my past the neighbor and I watched over the bones of creation that we ordered by the work of our womanly hands which contain the age-old knowledge of the architecture of joy and pain of the world The fragrant vapors rose up to the immense ceiling of the sky and warmed the mist-covered houses of Monticelli In the nostalgic and distant mystery of the Lombard landscape I told my daughter about the house on the canals that fanned out like long pale green hair in the landscape of docks and courtyard apartments Boats rested slow and quiet on the river water In those years I always saw men and women and children put one foot in front of the other as if the planet stayed up by itself planting their extremities on safe and solid ground and not on a bottomless void They bought butter pans TVs refrigerators computers insects lightbulbs typewriters They went to offices as money handlers and functionaries for the city the province the region Women cleaned house Children went to school to play to learn to live The planet stood on the precipice of the abyss while in the softness of the foggy Lombard landscape the deciduous queens of the sky dissolved into stardust frost hail ice Railing house apartments were always cold in the morning We would warm our frozen hands at the woodstove I liked the cold Some days my life in the North felt like exile It was a stopping place

I would eventually return to Naples or move to New York London Paris or some little town in Provence I loved France I would always eat croissants aux amandes like I did when I went with Santa to Suresnes where she went for a thyroid operation We were young and even bodily suffering faded in the delight of conversation and imagined futures that beckoned full of promises plans dreams After my husband's death I left Milan for this little town in the Po Lowlands where everyone knows everyone I got used to the landscape My daughter's father and I used to go on drives to Chiaravalle Vimodrone Vigevano with its beautiful castle and stables with majestic and stately colonnades It was a quiet life We didn't feel bourgeois We didn't put labels on things He went out in the morning and while I waited on teaching jobs I would order the bones of the house I dusted swept made the beds I was becoming a woman in chains Then I devoted myself to the handicrafts that had always been my mother's greatest skill I made wooden boxes that I hand-dyed and decorated with flowers dragons birds warriors elephants goats rams and frames and necklaces and salt dough figurines that I sold in boutiques I was proud of the money I earned on my own strengths and abilities In the afternoon I cooked for the evening Soups meatballs and spinach rice by mixing sautéed Italian rice and steamed chopped spinach with milk ricotta béchamel and fresh parmesan I didn't deny myself the pleasures of food Food is a God that commands generations It determines the uses and customs of peoples It observes shapes guides the lives of individuals Food is the God of the body—Reader—Occasionally friends came for dinner We would light a fire in the big fireplace we had built ourselves in the kitchen-living room of our apartment in the railing house where we knew everyone It was part of an old farmstead that used to have granaries and sheds and a well in the courtyard and a restaurant with an old sign saying "Da Rosa"

All was warm in the cold outside during those happy and complicated years We decorated the house with second-hand furniture from Trivulzio and street markets In the kitchen there was an antique credenza with a glass door through which shone plates and knickknacks and glasses a big chest from the early 1900s a table from the thirties and a simple wooden bed It was my fourth house How lovely and rustic it was When he died I cleaned out thirty years of life The empty frames cried out in silence while the dead leaves shone red on the deserted ground Throwing utensils clothes books photos randomly in boxes I realized I was in an everlasting ossuary I ordered the bones of my dead The dead yelled dreadfully with a rattling of bones and jaws not wanting to comply with the orders and desires of a leftover woman who like a vestal of times past toiled with the vacuum to reabsorb the dust of time into the bones to reconstruct the pages of the great book of memory by compiling the present past future of our little lives We all have equal honor in the eyes of God We have done what we could—my God—our hands know the cost of bread the cost of life the cost of paper the cost of sedatives the cost of patience the cost of hunger the cost of happiness the cost of heaven the cost of hell the cost of a star the cost of darkness the cost of living the cost of eating the cost of dying the cost of war the cost of peace the cost of paintings books newspapers roads bridges trees rivers women children the cost of looking the cost of touching the cost of the universe the cost of God the cost of salvation of perdition of guilt of innocence of a suitcase a hotel room the cost of a family the cost of a house the cost of a shotgun of rope of rigging the cost of being there of not being there the cost of being born of shouting of laughing of holding someone of killing them the cost of earth the trees the sea the cost of atoms prisons schools the cost of promenades parks gardens the cost of a continent the cost of a people the cost of accounting the cost of bills the cost of everything the final cost the cost of eternity

The dead quieted while my spine of iron and dead children's bones ached The funeral was gray in the big cemetery outside Pavia It was a gray rainy morning The sense and stench of death of must and wax hung in the air along the paths That leaden day lodged in my heart like a heavy lead wall in my life I see nothing but the word "nothing" written across the icosahedra of the sky That day I wrote in my journal "I am dead my God Love me Take me with you into your house Let us go down" A few days later I took my daughter and moved to Monticelli where at the sanitarium years ago I'd met the neighbor with her vacuum We stayed with her for a month until I found the little house along the state road where I live now in the foggy Lombard landscape of maples birches and poplars

For that night when I would reopen the restaurant I made us a light broth with risoni which my daughter loves We ate silently in the warm inside with the cold outside A fiendish hum spread through the neighborhood and the streets I could feel the whole town's eyes on me I turned the burners on under the clam sauce and fish soup I'd made that morning I put the water on for the spaghetti The fire in the fireplace glowed I uncorked bottles of wine and put sliced bread on the tables At seven thirty the first customers began to arrive It was a mellow couple in their seventies entrepreneurs in the local food industry Their eyes twinkled wickedly in the dull placidity of their faces The demon of food is the God of the body It contorts the features of our faces I filled the glasses with wine We had prepared a lavish banquet that would throw the order of the bones of creation into chaos The rich entrepreneurs from Varese and Brianza sipped the wine decorously Everyone was sitting and waiting for the food to appear

The big fat women and big Botero men sweated while I ordered the bones of my customers and of creation I put in the kitchen credenza the sweat-soaked bones exuding the infernal stench of the Brianza industrialist and his wife who like one of Botero's women arched her feet under the table and unfastened her corset and coat to reveal her big drooping bosom In the frenzy of the feast they gravitated down fat and decrepit The breasts of women—Reader—are harbors of longing and gulfs of certainty and beauty for the ships arriving from afar carrying their stowaways like shadows navigating through the chaos where creation is created matter materializes nature naturalizes and God godifies

Children in polka dot outfits and braids and bangs fought at the tables over chicken thighs and pork legs and pieces of cake like the white Caprese and chocolate Caprese I made in addition to the fish soup and spaghetti with clams and cockles and anchovies I also roasted whole chickens stuffed with thyme sage rosemary that I deboned and served with fried potatoes and roasted potatoes with thyme sage oil and rosemary and a puree of potatoes steamed and sieved with ricotta butter béchamel cheese egg and milk There was also a rich chicken broth I had simmered in a big pot with water celery carrot potato onion chard and escarole Then I skimmed the broth and put it aside it to pour over the tortelli I made by rolling out egg pasta dough into a thin layer and adding different fillings: ricotta and spinach and egg and ricotta pumpkin and radicchio and prosciutto and fresh cheese and egg I folded them up and left them to rest I served them with chicken broth and parmesan which I put in cheese dishes and bowls I'd made myself in the shape of ships and boats that resembled a little marine fleet like the one that lives in this sea finite flayed furrowed by ships carrying centuries gold millennia wines spices oils handicrafts freemen slaves This sea struck by waves by lights which never forgets a vessel a lighthouse a house This sea of buried dead And back come the millennia and centuries past the buried and reanimated dead and dark women hunched shrunken They weave cloth by the sea They wait rip stitch add rip hook gather They give substance to the sea A sea written drawn corporeal They make it the open closed body of the age-old sea barred with columns with vessels with lighthouses Sea of war sea of earth paper sea of flesh paper Egyptian Sicilian African sea Italian sea Sea of Spain France Greece Albania Roman sea inked handcrafted articulated sea fatigued never tired of setting forth Mediterranean

The children got dirty They stomped their feet They went to their mothers asking for food The mothers shooed them away giving them whatever they asked They were immersed in the inebriety of wine The children didn't figure Food is the God of the body—Reader—it determines the habits and customs of peoples who take its form and shape Food goes two ways It makes and is made It becomes part of the age-old soul and genetic and historical memory and the nucleus of every individual and people

The wine flowed in rivers that cascaded down my patrons' cavernous throats As I served the food with my daughter and neighbor with whom I ordered the bones we put the chicken bones and the children's bones and the bones of dinosaurs elephants giraffes insects and lightbulbs in the silverware drawers The old people's bones were buried under the embroidered linens I inherited from my mother who passed on to me the ancient wisdom of food that was contained in my hands

With our hands we go we pray we say we do we undo When I think of hands—Reader—I see my mother's hands busy with the daily toil of cooking and ordering the bones of creation I see my father's tired lined hands They'd handled fabrics for a lifetime testing textiles from the Jewish merchants in Lazio with whom he did business Ah the hands the hands!— Reader—they feel the hot the cold the soft the rough the slick the smooth Hands work hands rest in the lap of creation Our hands contain the brain and mind and soul and body and thought and the memory of all the many and the motley lives

The great feast continued The fiery fumes from the kitchen and hearth made the girls hike up their skirts The boys slid their vulgar hands underneath The women didn't speak In the imperious inebriety of food and drink all were afloat on the great sea of pleasure The whole street and the neighborhood gawked fiendishly from houses and courtyards in the Lombard landscape that's so dreamy in spring Now it was all fog and crime In the evening the air became a haze of fog and frost like hail and snow among the cross-stitch of maples poplars and birches that scattered the soil with needles lanceolate and pointed leaves that fell onto the rice fields The landscape was thunderous gold and green

I was nostalgic for the infinite expanse of olive trees where I went so often as a girl and shot at birds A thousand then a hundred then a thousand more fell to the ground I had buried my childhood after my grandmother died I made a grave in the dry earth and on top placed a cross at the junction of the abscissas of time and the ordinates of space It bled and bled The nails hurt The nails were fixed in the bones of man and God

The napkins fell to the floor in the second great feast in Monticelli where I had always ordered the bones of souls of things of creation

In the credenza with the napkins I put the bones of the icosahedra of the sky and the bones of the demons and angels of Anubis and Lethe and Demeter and Persephone and Astaroth and Christ and Buddha and Mohammed and Allah and my father and my mother and the bones of dead children the resurrected the lost the blessed the saved of history and the bones of Gentiles Protestants Catholics Franciscans Muslims and of Italians Germans Chinese that dance in the eternity of chaos in which dance the deciduous queens of heaven that over the restaurant Da Rosa fell like stardust in the form of fog and frost dewy with want

Outside the silence reigned translucent pearl and green like an aquarium traversed by the cold neon light from State Road 43 outlined against the backdrop of docks canals and channels scattered across the countryside hazy with fog and crimes in the lunar Lombard landscape Only the town of Monticelli glowed red extending its stores its traffic and commerce inhabited dark by the demons of food Flames flashed from my kitchen It was possessed by diabolic and angelic powers governing the God of food The infernal powers presided obscenely over the banquet There was one who had a head in the shape of an egg where his anus was supposed to be The effects of alcohol and food transformed the patrons They became figures in a Boschian carnival who attacked their food like a carnival piñata The women cradled their bellies swollen with food like the ancient Romans who vomited in order to eat again in a hopeless and endless cycle They devoured legs of lamb veal ox and pork that browned on the embers of the hearth The smell of roast from sea and earth wafted across the damned town blessed in its orgy of pleasure and pain It was the eternal ecstasy of food I cleaned the vomit in the bathrooms and continued ordering my patrons' bones I placed the bones of the children women and men on the shelves and in the drawers the industrialists from Varese and Brianza who were big fat and crude The children's bones were small like chicken bones The bones of creation rested on the insatiable hunger of the entire West concentrated in the restaurant that stood surrounded by rows of poplars maples and birch trees in a lunar landscape that contains the harmony of the celestial spheres and where the voice of chaos sings inside this sea finite flayed furrowed by ships carrying centuries gold millennia wines spices oils handicrafts freemen slaves This sea struck by waves by lights which never forgets a vessel a lighthouse a house This sea of buried dead And back come the millennia and centuries past the buried and reanimated dead and dark women hunched shrunken They weave cloth by the sea They wait rip stitch add rip hook gather They give substance to the sea A sea written drawn corporeal They make it the open closed body of the age-old sea barred with columns with vessels with lighthouses Sea of war sea of earth paper sea of flesh paper Egyptian Sicilian African sea Italian sea Sea of Spain France Greece Albania Roman sea inked handcrafted articulated sea fatigued never tired of setting forth Mediterranean

Even in the middle of the great feast I kept taking care of my patrons' bones I arranged them in the linen drawers I no longer distinguished between small and large I stuck them helter-skelter in the drawers and cabinets of my house which in time I had grown to love even though I was nostalgic for the infinite expanse of olive trees that I saw from the great distance of mature age which had led me to look at things with more detachment

The women unfastened their corsets and there were traces of vomit all over Once they headed out into the humid lust-red night the patrons I'd stuffed with fat scattered slow like a barbarian horde The whole crowd emerged from my house lost in the Padan fog like one sad newborn given over to the merciful arms of the night lost in the great hunger of the insatiable West A fescennine ceremony full of tragic spirit was being staged on the dark paths and State Road 43 Goats and tragoi and men thronged and danced mad together in a Boschian carnival of ruin while in the lost wind doves summoned by desire were answering a single cry It was love and compassion and mercy which are the eternal wisdom of the blessed and damned and saved of history Weary they walked one foot in front of the other in the landscape of the Po Lowlands full of fog and crime I knew that the great feast would recur The call of the senses and sex and food broke up the monotonous daily life of that corner of the world with carnivals of madness

With my daughter and neighbor I watched them disappear into a pale landscape as the furor reddened the pale sky We looked around the room littered with crumbs broken glass and oil stains The tablecloths were splattered with sauce and wine Crumpled napkins were strewn across the furniture and floor The embroidered white tablecloths were ruined Seeing precious items passed from generation to generation sullied was gutting I got them from my grandmother who had received them from her mother's hands as she had the jewelry box adorned with an eighteenth-century cameo of rare beauty The ancient knowledge of hands and food and cooking was morphing into an infernal art that awakened the wildest instincts of the rich and opulent populace of the Po Lowlands My innocent eatery and I were a lit fuse placed by chance in the lacustrine landscape of the Padan Plain The town waited to see my stove fire up to feel the urge for ultimate pleasure rekindle I never believed that this ancient and innocent knowledge would have been swept up in the waves of a mad destiny Adrift on my boat we staved off the waves of fate like breakers I too was prey to the collective delirium overtaking the West We looked around in a daze We picked up and cleaned until late Outside it was almost spring and a rain of fog and frost fell on the now quiet and rubescent lacustrine landscape with rows of maples poplars pines and canals We were incensed and tired of picking up and cleaning and scrubbing and washing You could smell orange and apple and mandarin peel under the embers That aroma took me back to my childhood Christmases when I would decorate the tree with little packages baubles lights and candles and put fruit peels on the fire and we roasted potatoes with salt and butter We'd only eaten pastina in broth We were hungry We had pastiera and milk and went to bed I saw my daughter's dark head on the pillow as she told me she was going to put up checked curtains in the Antibes house that I would see when I came to visit The image of Provence from my youth Happy I patted her and kissed her white forehead I would become a French grandmother We turned out the lights

The next morning I went back to work in the kitchen I too was prey to the collective madness I gathered all the leftover meat and made a mixture of beef veal chicken ox and sausage and made it into a giant meatloaf filled with rosemary eggs cheese ricotta and peas I baked it with butter oil sage and wine until it was golden brown I also made cutlets with milk by pan-cooking round steaks with milk salt onion butter and a splash of rum It was a dish I'd eaten many times as a child I also made some beef ravioli using the same egg pasta I'd rolled out on the counter I cut it into little squares I filled and sealed the ravioli and put them out to dry until the evening when I finished them with butter sage and milk

Upstairs my daughter was studying French and reading The neighbor at home deafened the rest of the town with her infernal vacuuming That pandemonium was the fuse that detonated the madness of the town whose hot points were the chock-full butcher shop my restaurant and the vacuum whose infinite and growling drone was the realm of time gone mad in the thunderous roar of death and life and all things over which rises the voice of chaos made of calm magma bliss and oblivion the chaos in which matter materializes nature naturalizes creation is created and God godifies

I worked away looking out at the soft Lombard landscape As I kneaded the dough I thought of the expanse of olive trees where I had lain so often as a girl I recalled the house where—after my mother died—I lived with my father It stood on the Hill of Remembrance with its gulfs and mossy caves trees and cliffs from which you could see the glowing red fires of the steel mill before it fell into disuse I heard the Phlegraean voice of the Cumaean Sibyl repeating "I want eternal life" I too wanted eternal youth I heard her voice trapped in the caves of Averno and Coroglio and Miseno repeating "I want to die" How could I have left behind that majestic and sublime landscape for flat foggy Lombardy? I had stopped asking myself that question I turned away from the past and dove back into my work I filled more squares with ricotta and cheese and fresh basil as the thunderous rumble of the vacuum cleaner jiggled the nails in the soul nailed at the junction of the abscissas of time and ordinates of space The nails hurt

The past weighed on me like a boulder that could start rolling at any moment A jumble of images appeared to me like one year—Naples 1956—when snow fell in the courtyard with its winged palms overlooking the Gulf of Naples in all its beauty and the whole bay with its islands was one of the most beautiful spots in the West whose insatiable hunger for ambition and power risked destroying the beauties of the known world and the entire universe I remembered being in the kitchen of my house in Naples with my brother We were kids We ate at a little table in the house on Via Tasso where we would sit while the adults sat in the dining room at the long marble table and we would get up from our spot to go steal the pudding our mother had put out on the terrace to cool Childhood is the beautiful and damned territory where the shape of our soul is forged I hung the laundered tablecloths out to dry still stained with wine Anxious but with my conscience at peace I went back to dicing the potatoes steamed with radicchio arugula lettuce chervil shallot tuna olives I went to iron the tablecloths I rested a while awaiting the evening I feared a third bacchanal I ordered the bones of creation that lay mad and secret in the Lombard landscape In the trees I placed the bones of children and small animals In the sky I placed the bones of the dead in the grass the bones of our forebears In the dirt my own

My daughter came downstairs We ate together The table was dressed with a tablecloth handed down from my great-grandmother that I had saved from the revelry She told me about her house It was a house in Antibes overlooking the sea Out the windows you could see sailboats It was a big open space with a separate area for the bathroom and for a small bedroom You could see the soft French hills of Provence outside After breakfast I went to the stove as I was going to open that night I could already feel and smell the third great feast in the air

That night full of want I saw hordes of men and women swarming the trattoria Da Rosa clad in indigo to every color of the rainbow: Prussian blue petrol green pitch black baby blue rose dawn fire red carmine royal purple like angelic and celestial powers spread through the landscape of moorland

63

and canals and docks and dams and jetties where the harmony of chaos sings in which matter materializes creation is created things thingify And God godifies

While I prepared sausages and roasts putting veal beef ox chicken pork shanks on the fire I made a vitel tonnè by steaming paper-thin slices of veal and covering them in a sauce of mayonnaise blended with tuna capers olives and parsley I stepped away from the kitchen and in my journal jotted down the shopping list for souls In the restaurant that night the big Botero women wore tight corsets and tight long pleated skirts under which they wore garters and stockings in black and gold and silver and dark violet and nude and baby blue Men stuck fat hands between fat and thin thighs Like a bunch of Don Juans they didn't discriminate between fat thin scrawny chubby old or young or adolescent They had a list like Leporello: Austrian French Italian old pretty blond brunette To them they were the same

In the fires of the room the faces of the stony feasters shone with grease and furor I served them the meat that disappeared in chunks down gaping maws The bread was swallowed up by voracious mouths The roasts exuded their scents and their sauces from the dining room to the soft Lombard landscape outside the window Now and then my daughter would tell me about the house in Antibes with its checked curtains and striped tablecloths in white and blue and indigo and violet and sky blue and olive green and Prussian blue "My child" I said "don't make shopping lists for souls Love your man without servitude without reserve without leftovers without resentments without hate without regrets Cast off your chains Give yourself over to death in your life" Oh the chains—Reader— they tug at the hearts and limbs of entire generations and all peoples of the earth at home on the street in the labor camps in the concentration camps Ah! Chains are skeins of endless suffering and pain Chains squeeze the throat they suffocate They are death's name—Reader—

My daughter gave me a hand She was covered in sweat The sweat poured off the brow of my young girl in flower projected toward a future of want Now and then we ate bread and gnawed at the bones We were seized by the disorder that possessed us The restaurant was the focal point of a universe of instinct and want The roasts lay splayed on the tables with Mediterranean herbs inside It was meat for slaughter I recalled the butcher shop below our house in Naples when I was little The quarters of ox of lamb the rabbits the suckling pigs kid goats chickens hens were butchered alive like the animals the railworkers and farmhands in Crespi d'Adda brought to the butcher's They would be weighed and then you—Reader—saw the suffering animals shackled to be led to the axe that would cut them down The blood pooled black like Odysseus's which he drank before setting off on his journey to the underworld on the everlasting Lethe He embraced the heroes and the beloved shade of his mother Anticlea Ah the shades Shadows—Reader—are reality Everything depends on reality—Reader—Shadows are the stowaways we carry below deck on our ship that sails this sea finite flayed furrowed by ships carrying centuries gold millennia wines spices oils handicrafts freemen slaves This sea struck by waves by lights which never forgets a vessel a lighthouse a house This sea of buried dead And back come the millennia and centuries past the buried and reanimated dead and dark women hunched shrunken They weave cloth by the sea They wait rip sew add rip hook gather They give substance to the sea A sea written drawn corporeal They make it the open closed body of the age-old sea barred with columns with vessels with lighthouses Sea of war sea of earth paper sea of flesh paper

Egyptian Sicilian African sea Italian sea Sea of Spain France Greece Albania Roman sea inked handcrafted articulated sea fatigued never tired of setting forth Mediterranean

They sank their teeth into legs of lamb and slices of cake like stones and sheets to be ground in their voracious mouths The Monticelli butcher was a fiend He dug into his own lamb legs his chicken roulades and meatballs They all ate from the pot of heaven out of which poured every kind of manna upon humanity

As crumbs and wine dropped on the floor we had just cleaned my mind returned to the infinite expanse of olive trees with all its splendor and pungent southern scent where one day I encountered the Nazarene with his chalice of wine and ricotta on top of the stone that buried my childhood which I buried after my grandmother died The Nazarene didn't want to drink his chalice made from the flesh and blood of humans and God

My hands were busy in the kitchen mixing leftover pieces of lamb with potatoes to make a savory puree I couldn't turn my business into a ruin I was scared of ruins With a mix of angst excitement and pleasure I looked at the group of civilized barbarians at Da Rosa Rosa was my name I gave it to myself It shone on the side of my ship that furrowed the back of the seas in the squall the storm the squall the sirocco The trattoria sailed between the tropics and the equator I saw the ship of my life made of solitude go alone into the horizon parallel with the ships of all the mad the drowned the saved of history

Suddenly in the bacchanal the vacuum of the demons and of God let out a howl It was an apocalyptic seal on human pleasure The neighbor had turned to it to replace the God of the body and the God of food with another It was the God of time that led to madness in the mind and the clocks whose infernal tick-tock plagued the cannibalistic orgy of the big fat provincial industrial bourgeoisie of the Po Lowlands The vacuum went on in her life of suffering and want Its deafening shriek invaded the soft and gentle Lombard plain

After the bacchanal we were tired we would clean up tomorrow With my head resting on a pillow next to my sweet daughter's my mind returned to the trip to Naples and the coast I'd wanted to take for so long But I was scared to face the past I saw the wild and intense landscapes of sheer cliffs that plunge into the sea and I felt the violent wind hitting my face the way it did when I was a girl walking down Via Petrarca and Via Manzoni in the gusty mist That sylvan and sublime landscape frightened me as much as encountering the faces and façades of the past Only continuous presence ensures continuity between past and present and doesn't distort the past images of an entire life Maybe that trip wasn't a good idea I recalled my brother's house where we would go because in Naples and on the coast—after selling the family home—my only place to stay was with my brother or with friends I recalled the long hallway leading to the bedrooms in one of which I stayed for Christmas after the sanitarium in Monticelli I recalled the kitchen where on many mornings I ate cookies for breakfast quietly waiting for the house to awaken Then my sister-in-law and I would go out around Naples and visit the Certosa di San Martino One morning we went to Virgil's tomb which was high up the tufa paths on the hill of Posillipo We looked at the plaques and the grave inscriptions It was a raging and wild landscape of vigor and desire

She suggested we tour Naples underground but I was afraid of succumbing to panic and claustrophobia wandering through those immense subterranean gorges full of tombs and Greek baths and deposits from the Second World War and smugglers' contraband One morning my brother my daughter my niece and I went to Pozzuoli to visit the Rione Terra with its castle and tombs in the crypts of Gothic churches The main piazza was small and pretty There were cafés and restaurants and pizzerias It wasn't so different from the village landscapes of Provence I'd visited with my husband At my brother's in the morning after breakfast I went into the bathroom where the potent sunlight beat down even in winter I showered under the powerful jets of water that warmed me up as I've always been prone to cold I could hear my nieces who were getting ready for their classes at the university One was blond the other brunette They were pretty Laura kept my homemade handicrafts in her room It was full of little figurines depicting black-painted legs and faces cut off as if by a scythe Now that jumble of images from the past scared me Maybe I could go after taking a break from the nightly orgies and restaurant work which I wouldn't give up because it had become my occupation I recalled my brother's cozy living room with pictures of him as well as of my daughter and grandparents and nieces and also of me and my husband From its great big windows you could see the houses across the way with their windows and verandas with white tile borders and in the middle up on the Vomero hill where the Via Cammarano house was the funicular ran and you could see the trees heavy with oranges on which shone the absolute light of things that exist even without being seen It was the same light that shone on the tablecloths that had belonged to my grandmother and mother

Resting my head on the pillow I drifted off thinking of Santa's house and Marina's house Santa's house had stairs like the circles of hell spiraling upward in a shell or double helix in which sings the voice of chaos in which creation is created matter materializes nature naturalizes things thingify And God godifies

From the windows with a view of Vico Santa Teresella degli Spagnoli down to Castel Sant'Elmo and the Certosa di San Martino that shone under the deciduous queens of heaven that hover over this sea finite flayed furrowed by ships carrying centuries gold millennia wines spices oils handicrafts freemen slaves

Down in the streets of the Spanish Quarter the usual theater of war unfolded You had to see it—Reader—mozzarella makers fishmongers fruit sellers office workers housewives fabric merchants getting all worked up over fish glistening with seaweed and mussels Snails and tuna and octopuses swam in the cold morning water that Christmas when I went down to Naples and stayed at my brother Maurizio's There were white milky mounds of mozzarella There were sprigs of mistletoe tucked between bolts of fabric And the silks and the tweeds and the satins and the cottons and the linens and the brocades lustered in their buyers' hands It was a marvelous market which we looked at in awe while at Santa's house we looked out at the nativity scenes from San Gregorio Armeno down below Precious porcelain angels hung on old aristocratic ceilings crumbling with age As I remembered that wonderful Christmas from my kitchen in the Po Lowlands I felt all the weight of the past I wasn't ready to face what had been I let myself be carried away by the hazy image of Santa's hands and the nativities There were also a hundred and a hundred then a thousand and a hundred thousand shepherds of wonder and magi with their camels and servants and chicken cages and chickens and baskets of fruit and terracotta and baskets of bread fish eggs grapes oranges mandarins tomatoes peppers eggplants cabbages broccoli and lemons and lemon sellers and stands with grains and sausages all bearing their marvelous array of food and flowers and fruit

On the street the incessant theater of war unfolded on that street in turn full of stands selling fish grain fabric walnuts candied oranges almonds and Christmas struffoli and mostaccioli and roccocò and cassata and glasses and plates and cups and other Christmas items whose geometry of decumans and centurias recalled the piazzas and streets of Pozzuoli and the streets and squares of Provence like in Antibes where I would go visit my daughter once she left home

I preferred to cultivate these images of futurity rather than sink into those of the past I didn't think I would make our trip to Amalfi The past weighed on me I began to feel a growing distance in my soul from the deafening roar of the vacuum which was the town of Monticelli's God of time Eternal time in its fixed and immobile power and time marked by the hours and the tick-tock of the clocks heightened the disorder and madness which is the dark side of the chaos that sings in this sea finite flayed furrowed by ships carrying centuries gold millennia wines spices oils handicrafts freemen slaves This sea struck by waves by lights which never forgets a vessel a lighthouse a house This sea of buried dead And back come the millennia and centuries past the buried and reanimated dead and dark women hunched shrunken They weave cloth by the sea They wait rip sew add rip hook gather They give substance to the sea A sea written drawn corporeal They make it the open closed body of the age-old sea barred with columns with vessels with lighthouses Sea of war sea of earth paper sea of flesh paper Egyptian Sicilian African sea Italian sea Sea of Spain France Greece Albania Roman sea inked handcrafted articulated sea fatigued never tired of setting forth Mediterranean

And the seed of a sibilant black madness sprouted inside me and it would stay with me till the end of the story I needed some relief from the madness I'd just go for a stay at the

Monticelli sanitarium as my one getaway and vacation to relieve the fatigue from the kitchen where I practiced the sacred and blessed art that my mother passed down to me that was contained in my hands I recalled my mother's hands and my daughter's hands and my neighbor's hands and Santa's and Marina's They were the hands of women who had worked touched cooked sewn mended opened closed pointed shown covered provided loved Forever For all eternity

On that Neapolitan Christmas Santa and I stepped away from the balcony overlooking the terrace filled with plants and flowers hibiscus spider plants geraniums amaranth crown-of-thorns daisies anemones forget-me-nots and bluebells The terrace was black and blue with water from the pots and the wispy fog in the sky Sparse clouds dotted the calm breeze over that Neapolitan nativity Santa smiled with the enigmatic and sad face of a woman deeply alone even though she had a daughter a son and a husband I watched her stand in the center of the compass rose on the terracotta tiles on the floor Beneath her feet as beneath my mother's the compass rose converged with all the directions of the earth nailed to the cross of the ordinates of time and abscissas of space We went to sit in the many-windowed living room with gray-blue armchairs and sofas books pottery she made with her own hands by shaping clay into cups plates bowls teapots fruit bowls goblets that she decorated with earth pigments and fired at a nearby kiln and little bowls with embedded shells Shells were also arranged on the ground and in crystal orbs all over She also made decorative tiles painted in white blue orange and gold like tufa As a gift she gave me a wide-mouthed bowl whose gray-veined center showed a white blue purple gray octopus in bas-relief biting through the surface like a tentacular flower In that octopus which is now in the Monticelli kitchen I glimpsed the outline of that madness fomented by the tremendous roar of the neighbor's vacuum which along with the orgiastic fires was the seed of negligence and disorder and disease and pleasure all at once Human things are complex Evil is always embedded in good and disorder in harmony

That morning after the third great feast the neighbor fired up the vacuum of madness first to clean my house then hers with repetitive and maniacal urgency The whole town restless and undone after the revelry and intoxication and extreme lassitude of the sins of lust and gluttony perked up at that sibilant and mad roar eternal and serpentine that was the figure of time passing without return The word "nevermore" was stamped on the waves of the sky that ran onto the surface of the seas The word "nevermore" like the stowaway that was dead time time's cadaver dragged from equator to tropics all the way to the center of the compass rose where past present and future cancel each other out and forever lives for all eternity

Back in Naples Santa handed me her gift as her children and husband came in We sat at the table to eat mozzarella bread ricotta and sausage and rapini prepared by mixing salt oil and garlic with the bitter wilted greens served with traditional thin Neapolitan sausages poached golden and pierced to release excess liquid and fat It was simple and hearty food which we ate in silence in harmony with ourselves and with creation The scent of pine and mandarin and orange and the fire burning with the citrus peels wafted sweet and inviting through the house overlooking the Spanish streets and the panorama of all Naples All Neapolitan houses stand on tufa cliffs and escarpments whose roots sink into a hollow composed of caverns tombs Greek baths leftover weapons from the Second World War and stashes of contraband cigarettes and drugs When the earth quakes in that hollow so do its arms sunken into Naples into the age-old tufa underground hollow When the earth quakes men and women go pale with creeping terror awaiting the awakening of the tremendous Volcano the eternal exterminator that rules the lives of Neapolitans and looms over the land from Torre del Greco to Coroglio to Lake Avernus to Miseno to Bacoli to the Phlegraean Fields to the Nola countryside threatening to destroy arches temples palaces towers bridges Greek and Roman temples aqueducts architraves churches Try to imagine—Reader—seeing the façade of the royal palace quake in a violent tremor from the turbulent bowels of the earth and then crumble to the ground into the dust of time flattening the royal statues of the Bourbons the Austrians of Philip II of Spain and Charles of Anjou and Conradin of Swabia into the dust of time as the anomalous wave from a seaquake slams the port making ships and boats and tools and hulls and rocks and stones and concrete collide with a thunderous screech and crash into the shores of Coroglio and the Phlegraean Fields and the Nola countryside

As we sat and ate I dug down in the hollow Pierced by the raging and extreme beauty of my native landscape I could feel its horrid beauty at my back I approached that extreme landscape with trepidation I was used to the flat and serene landscape of the Lombard plains without extremes without force without vigor abandoned in its faint mists like a sleeping woman in the night of time

After lunch Marina came and took me to her house Now that I'm reliving that past I realize that with my cooking I've released the extreme madness of the southern landscape within the Lombard landscape of mist fog and crime that dwells in revelry and the flames of the stove and the oven and the hearth and the food that ignites the spirits and extreme instincts pent up in the bellies hearts heads of the opulent Padan bourgeoisie

The madness that always centuplicates in the vacuum's thunderous rumble

My daughter was out at the university in Pavia I was alone in the kitchen and I could feel the likelihood of colliding with the overwhelming landscape of the past wane I was satisfied with the madness of the age-old knowledge of food and cooking contained within my hands The madness of food revived the deafening roar of the God of time that lived in revelry and the clocks' tick-tock We'll all of us die from the madness of clocks

I turned back to the past I didn't know where to look to find relief from the burden of the strong and tenacious and extreme memories of the South I recalled Marina and her Botticellian face with our daughters at Santa's house We had coffee together and nibbled on Caprese cake Marina brought me to her house that spiraled over Toledo That house stood on a steep cliff too In its sheer fullness the entire city cultivated the fullness of emptiness It is a great city in which sings this sea finite flayed furrowed by ships carrying centuries gold millennia wines spices oils handicrafts freemen slaves This sea struck by waves by lights which never forgets a vessel a lighthouse a house This sea of buried dead And back come the millennia and centuries past the buried and reanimated dead and dark women hunched shrunken They weave cloth by the sea They wait rip sew add rip hook gather They give substance to the sea A sea written drawn corporeal They make it the open closed body of the age-old sea barred with columns with vessels with lighthouses Sea of war sea of earth paper sea of flesh paper Egyptian Sicilian African sea Italian sea Sea of Spain France Greece Albania Roman sea inked handcrafted articulated sea fatigued never tired of setting forth Mediterranean

We traversed the narrow streets pitched on the steep slope passing the low homes in whose windows appeared dark women and raggedy children and angels with golden swords in the middle of the wild infernal wood of scooters shopkeepers bottegas hawkers All along the upsloping street and sharp drops the fishmongers' fish glistened Their wares with their metallic and silver and blue-green colors glittered in the metallic Neapolitan sun which beamed supreme and funereal over the fates of an entire people We walked intent on ourselves without speaking The girls followed behind in silence Serene we put one foot in front of the other going up and down We ambled over cobblestones poking up from the ground past Vanvitelli and sixteenth-century and seventeenth-century and Baroque façades and by the Palazzo Serra di Cassano We came to the stairs to her house which spiraled in a helix in the exposed tufa surrounded by stolen motorcycle parts and hanging laundry that smelled of bleach and lye Everywhere the ancient walls were crumbling in the hothouse of Naples' eternal air crackling with furor We climbed the stairs and crossed a narrow gate leading to a house so tall it seemed to stand on the tallest rampart of the sky

Marina's house was perched on a mountain of sky that rose up on the roof of the world with rows of bluebells grapevines hibiscus geraniums anemones petunias peacock flowers You entered through a very tall door leading to a large space with one central room overlooking Sant'Elmo and the Certosa di San Martino

In a corner there were the girls' toys a mountain of Barbies stuffed cats peacocks zebras giraffes elephants mammoths animals of every species in creation which lives in the voice of chaos in which nature naturalizes matter materializes things thingify and God godifies The variegated parquet reflected the colors of the sky that rose high above the insatiable Western hunger in the room where we sat on the bed and she reached her hand out to mine in a lesbian caress tapping into that vein of madness brought out by the disorder that lives in the madness of food and the vacuum which together with the frenzied pace of the hours condemns everyone to death Her hands caressed me gently more gently than a man's I accepted that relationship as a natural experience in my life devoid of men and having truly loved only my mother who had passed down to me the age-old knowledge of food The rooms faded into the maze of the contorted courtyards over the lanes of Toledo the old Spanish streets overlooking the sea In the room where we lay on the bed her hand caressed my pubis and my breasts We were two free women loving each other without resentment without waste without regret without pain At times seized by the seed of madness that lives in the disorder of time my thoughts went to the gun I kept in my nightstand drawer I'd packed it for that Christmas trip to Naples Above us outstretched in bed as friends like limp odalisques the sky shone over a terrace as high as the ramparts of the sky in which we saw ships and ships go by the thousand and a hundred and a thousand more It was a slanted and rectangular terrace that looked like the anus of the sky My hand went to Marina's small sweet breasts as her small squat girlish hand caressed my pubis Oblivious to children husbands relatives friends and all past and future generations Then nearly naked we went to the little kitchen with a skylight where the ramparts of the sky loomed We prepared milk and cookies bread and butter and jam we poured tea in one of Santa's pots In the pans sat the fried chicken Marina had made by placing strips of chicken breast and thigh in boiling oil after coating them in egg and flour There was also rice sautéed with oil garlic onion and butter and meatballs in a tomato ragù made by simmering garlic oil basil onion celery potato carrot butter and tomato for an hour We tasted them in the disorder that was about to take over our minds Then we went back to bed and curled up in the sheets as if in a shroud of desire We cradled our lesbian love in which lived a vein of slight sweet desperate madness which along with the madness of temporal disorder already followed me wherever I heard the clocks' tick-tock and the vacuum cleaner's roar Our hands sought each other like little ships going toward their fate by the thousand They were flowers of longing that blossomed in our love-hungry hands that went searching for the oblivion the bliss the nothingness that belong to God In the sheet-shroud hands touched ears and nose and mouth and hips Our skin was caressed all over by these hands that know the cost of bread the cost of life the cost of death the cost of paper the cost of sedatives the cost of patience the cost of hunger the cost of happiness the cost of heaven the cost of hell the cost of a star the cost of darkness the cost of living the cost of eating the cost of dying the cost of war the cost of peace the cost of paintings books newspapers streets bridges trees rivers women children the cost of looking the cost of touching the cost of the universe the cost of God the cost of salvation of perdition of guilt of innocence of a suitcase of a hotel room the cost of a family the cost of a house the cost of a rifle of rope of rigging the cost of being there of not being there the cost of being born of crying of laughing of hugging someone of killing someone the cost of land trees sea the cost of atoms prisons schools the cost of boulevards parks gardens the cost of a continent the cost of a people the cost of accounting the cost of the bill the cost of everything the final cost the cost of eternity They were a woman's hands a man's a little girl's They metamorphosed into love our women's hands that contained the age-old knowledge of food of time of love of art and of cooking If my hand went to the gun Marina's

hand stopped it It was an imperious hand that commanded
love compassion pleasure and oblivion instead of the theater
of war that unfolded in the streets of Naples The hand poised
on the gun paused Its fingers sought her pubis as she looked
at me with smoldering eyes She was a Botticellian creature
We rolled in the sheets in the gray and blue and purple blankets as my mind drifted to the kitchen in Monticelli to the
roast to prepare for the certain next great feast whose scent
already rose over the rubescent roofs of Padania I recalled her
hands and I recalled myself with her in the kitchen on Vico
Lungo Pontecorvo whose steep slopes mounted the ramparts
of the sky its high clouds hazy with foreboding My mind kept
returning to the gun but the loving hand stopped it Lazily we
went back to eat It was such sweet food we nibbled happy to
be without waste or reservations or regrets nor guilt nor pain
We were permeated by the fullness of our lesbian love We went
to bathe together running our hands over our wet skin in the
chilly bathroom where the steam fogged up the glass and the
majolica tiles with blue purple yellow and gold flowers Serene
we went to bed at the same time as the girls In a light sleep my
hand ventured onto her breast We lay under a blanket of stars
From the big window overlooking the port we saw oil tankers
in the rubescent light of the clouds of a metallic winter sunset
over Naples We watched the ships go by carrying the stowaway
on board like everyone's shadow We also saw the shadow in
our relationship which would sometimes be tormented by an
unconfessed guilt I saw the ship named Rosa sailing toward
its destiny Rosa was my name I gave it to myself Our hands
searched for each other in a sleep that turned fitful Every love
between women is tormented tenebrous happy and unhappy
You navigate an abyss of good and bad made of impetuous
impulses sweet and absolute Every so often my mind would go

back to the gun Marina's hand diverted it She kept me from any extreme act We went back to the kitchen to snack some more Then in the middle of the night while the girls slept we went to use the age-old knowledge of food and made pasta and broccoli by sautéing boiled broccoli in oil and garlic and mixing it with tagliatelle and hot pepper Then we made a quick brioche for the girls by mixing eggs sugar flour egg cocoa yeast and starch We baked it for half an hour and dusted it with powdered sugar We cleaned up and went back to bed The wisdom of cooking could produce sweet light foods to be eaten in harmony or it could unleash base and unchecked impulses like the debauchery incited in the town of Monticelli in my Padan kitchen in the immeasurable distance from those Neapolitan years Already I could see the flames from the stove rising into the sky

I took my mind off the burden of the past That lesbian love had filled the holes in my soul and if the neighbor hadn't hounded me with her mad vacuum I would have sought a relationship with her too I love all women—Reader—I sleep alone I seek women out of a need for gratuitous and total affection and to escape my bed where I sleep alone in the provincial isolation of the Po Lowlands I decided to find more women and as I was cooking I thought that women in Padania were fat and vulgar business wives and mothers devoted to nothing but shopping and clothes

I decided to play the Don Juan Fat thin pretty ugly young old didn't matter to me I went to make a roast beef browning an eye of round with sage oil butter thyme rosemary and milk and a little rum with a side of zucchini carrots potatoes rabe green beans with garlic and tomato and a carbonara which I made by mixing egg parmesan ricotta and cubes of prosciutto sausage and mozzarella for the tagliatelle I had made that morning I added rum to make the simple dish rich and fiendish

I knew that after Marina no love with a woman would be total and absolute yet it would be a less impetuous impulsive and passionate bond to fill the bed where I sleep alone I thought of the neighbor who was my age I went to her and made her turn off her infernal vacuum I took her to my room where I let down her blond-gray hair and I removed her maniacal dress and apron I gave her a black dress of mine embroidered with violet and purple and fire-red roses For an instant of eternal silence we looked out at the silent Padan landscape of fog crime and canals against a sky pale with frost Tina was upset She took off the dress It didn't suit her It didn't suit her soul She was right I couldn't remake her to my will The woman understood and took my hand pulling me to the bed Softly our hands searched each other with innocent wordless caresses I was a lesbian By now I knew I didn't care what my neighbors or patrons would say We stayed under the covers for two hours without words without cares in the cosmos-sheet where life is frescoed Then we each went back to our own world she to the cleaning and the muted madness of the vacuum that drove me insane and I into the madness of food In the kitchen I saw in the food and the thunderous rumble the hosts of hell dancing to the beat of a mad Sabbath as if Bosch's demons had come together in a giant carnival It was a mix of madness hate and love I wanted a quiet life I prayed to my God to silence the madness of clocks and bad time in me I busied my hands with a stew of potatoes peas carrots chickpeas greens chard green beans and ground meat It was a fat supper fated to unleash the hunger of the insatiable West in that corner of world in the Po Lowlands That night just before eight patrons began to arrive in pairs I saw among them the beautiful wife of a wealthy industrialist whom I liked right away I was ready to trade in the neighbor for her I was eager for a new love They sat down at the tables with my mother's embroidered tablecloths which despite the lye and bleach still showed traces of sauce and wine With the neighbor looking at me with tenderness and jealousy and my daughter who knew nothing about any of it we served pasta alla carbonara

The patrons dove into their plates filling their bottomless bellies Food is good—Reader—They drank but ungreedily I looked at the beautiful woman whose hands were folded in her lap I went over I asked her if she wanted more pasta or bread or wine I wanted to meet her hear her voice I wanted to know about her life She was young and pretty She had the features of a Botero woman: small sinuous mouth tiny ears narrow eyes These strange features mixed with a Greek nose made for an uncommon and striking physiognomy I offered her the best morsels: cutlets in butter chicken thighs braised in rum wine and cream It was a rich and inviting dish She didn't conceal her almost ancestral desire for food she could satisfy as she pleased because she was the wife of a rich industrialist from Brianza transplanted to foggy Padania Her body was small and sinuous She looked like a plastic doll It was her almost artificial beauty that evoked one of those spiritless soulless willless inflatable dolls you could buy in the fifties in America the industrialized West and Japan to make aseptic and one-sided love to The marvelous thing about this woman is she was a flesh and blood doll Her husband looked at her with concupiscent eyes full of possessiveness and domination That real doll of real flesh was his He had bought her He had bought her soul with his money his power that allowed him to satisfy all her whims Clearly he showered her with furs and expensive clothes That night she was wearing a snug black dress that showed off her round hips and tiny waist her slender ankles her hearty calves and thighs She was a woman without a soul I had a child's soul in a woman's body In my heart yearning for feminine tenderness she was the ideal replacement for the neighbor who was advanced in years like me She was my age we were peers But with this woman I could play the man or the mother although I didn't want roles or fictions I wanted to be myself with all my desperate need for love that pushed me toward the total gratuity of women I glimpsed from afar like ports of longing I watched her eat I didn't take my eyes off her table She looked at me too as if she suspected my lascivious intentions She looked at me with mischievous and amused eyes Maybe saw my desire with pity but I didn't want pity or compassion I wanted a relationship between equals I was a tall and well-aged woman and still active even too much so All that activity perhaps led me to desire as a harbor for my ship tossed by the waves of fate a port between a woman's legs Ultimately men had just been the other half of the sky in my life Now I wanted women alone

I kept circulating among the tables where the orgy of wine meat and fish continued Plates came one after the other I had already served the meat and vegetable stew and the carbonara with the fresh egg tagliatelle I'd made early that morning

Now and then as I went around the tables images from the past took hold of me There was Marina with her body as a peer and friend My mother the only true great love of my life on whose lap I rested my tired head when she was in bed in the morning I never dared touch my mother who seemed profaned by the touch of my father who seemed like an extraneous figure beside her and in her bed when we gathered to watch TV at night in their bedroom and sometimes my mother would get up and under her thin nightgowns you could see her form tall and willowy but droopy with age My mother was modest She covered up with a robe as if she could feel her children's eyes on her These were magical and dramatic moments when our mother was in bed instead of the kitchen where she had passed down to me her age-old knowledge of food

All the women later in my life were nothing but simulacra of my mother who with her divinity as a sacred Madonna and kore reigned over our lives in the house on Via Tasso where we lived when we were little and where her body loomed full of promise and futurity We watched her in the courtyard with the winged palms when Assunta was out hanging the laundry and she came to the window to tell us not to stay out late Her voice took us back to the warmth of round sweet-smelling pastries and the soups and stews and roasts with which she constellated our childhood to make it good and pleasant along with the smell of the fire sending smoke and ash into the sky which in winter meant her monachine pastries My mother was a screen-woman like in Dante Behind her stood the heavens of the Lord Every other woman in my life had to bear some trace of her be her opposite like the plump little Botero sitting at a table in my restaurant Da Rosa Her antagonist by negating her rendered her present in my mind but at the same time detoxified me from that eternal intoxication that my mother's life had been in mine

I kept making the rounds of the tables with my daughter and our neighbor Tina who maybe to please me was wearing a dark flowered dress Tina was watching me She realized I was eyeing the young woman at table six Tina carried a dish of sausages and roasts served with beans and fresh vegetables in a dressing of oil mayonnaise capers anchovies and olives that sat atop steamed cauliflower roses encircled by roundels of carrot and beet and lemon wedges and a big plate of roasted potatoes Tina tiredly set the big plate at the edge of table six The pretty little woman scooped herself an abundant serving under her husband's greedy eyes They helped themselves to pies filled with meat and béchamel and cheese and ricotta and peas and spinach that I had made from a dough of flour salt water and yeast that I mixed and cooked in a bain-marie until it rose I arranged single portions on a baking tray lined with foil They came out as little stuffed puffs With the same dough I made sweet zeppole With a pastry bag I shaped the dough into little roses which expanded in the oven Some I fried in oil In the middle like a woman's pubis I placed the pale cream and dark cherry blood The zeppole's gluttonous and sensual allure attracted the greedy gaze of the rich industrialist who devoured them with his eyes the way he devoured his wife's round and turgid little breasts She too helped herself greedily Her sweet beady eyes softened with pleasure as she devoured the meat pies from the tines of her fork I also made a roast en croute I wrapped a tender round of veal in dough kneaded out of flour egg water salt and oil until it became a smooth and silky dough I rolled out the same pastry and made savory pies and I cut the veal en croute into sumptuous slices glorious with aroma and flavor It was filled with ricotta and spinach and peas I looked at the beautiful woman's greedy little mouth her pearl teeth unabashedly sinking in

My daughter noticed me staring at the beautiful woman Maybe for the first time she felt jealous She realized that by following her own path she could lose her mother I looked through all the women in my life: my daughter Marina Santa my mother In each I saw a different beauty We are each ourselves in the eyes of God Like pines at my window those woman figures rose against the sky of longing of the Lombard lowlands which extinguished the fires of my patrons' nightly binges I saw the ship with the name Rosa on the side It was my name I gave it to myself And I saw processions of coffin after coffin heading into the horizon of the Padan landscape of fog and crime My mind went back to the sanitarium above Monticelli where I would go to assuage the madness of food and revelry and the glorious weight of my lesbian love entirely of woman for the whole world that was the gift and the guilt of my life I felt threatened somehow and not present enough for my daughter But she had her path and her French future We were free and equal in the eyes of the world and of God I looked back at the beautiful woman and her dark hair I would invite her to go out I wanted to know everything about her Privately I played the part of Don Juan which didn't suit me It was just a mask placed over my face strained with desire and longing I didn't want to possess or conquer or dominate I didn't want to be a man I didn't have a man's mask inside my soul I'm just a woman—Lord—I sleep alone At night when I go to bed in my lonely sheets that gape like a shroud empty of hands I feel lost Lord tell me you still love me Love me forever for all eternity in the waves of the cosmos-sheet where life is frescoed I feel alone and lost, my God My talent can't save me Nor am I sustained by the ancient wisdom passed from my mother into my hands that lie bare and alone in the bed where I sleep alone Love me God Love me forever For all eternity

My lonely woman's eyes went timid as I truly am The Don Juan mask fell but I have no regrets my God I have loved only women This I will bring as a gift to my dead and my living and lay at the foot of God's throne when I die—Lord—I will bring my glorious domesticitude cultivated in all those nights of longing in the dormant heart of the world of the Po Lowlands and that is written like all lives and deaths on the cosmos-sheet where life is frescoed I gave pleasure—my God—it wasn't a sin When I die I'll bring my living and my dead all the struffoli tarts beignets savory pies fried pizzelle that I learned from

my mother's age-old art I'll lay at the feet of the angels and
God my roasts my stews broccoli pasta wine-braised sausages cassata roccocò mostaccioli pasta with ragù pasta with
pesto sautéed vegetables stuffed chickens and turkeys hen
in broth with celery carrot and potato stuffed suckling pig
thrush with polenta rapini with garlic Olivier salad vitel tonnè
shrimp cocktail green salad mayonnaise vegetables agrodolce
stuffed peppers eggplant mushroom-style with tomatoes and
garlic and eggplant-zucchini parmesan with mozzarella tomato
and parmesan and roasted peppers in oil garlic and parsley
meat-stuffed zucchini broth with butter fried chicken roasted
chicken goose au gratin pork cutlets with rosemary-roasted
potatoes and boiled potatoes and cannoli made with dough
wrapped around metal tubes fried and filled with silky ricotta
mixed with melted sugar candied fruit chocolate chips and
wheat berries pastiera made with ricotta and orange blossom
and sponge cake layered with pastry cream and chocolate
cream I will lay at the feet of God and the feet of my living
and my dead T-bone steaks and chicken cutlets and veal cutlets and sautéed beef liver with golden onions and grilled
pork liver cooked in caul fat with rosemary thyme and sage
browned in oil butter and onion and green bean potato salad
and San Marzano tomato salad with anchovies salt oil parsley oregano olives and cubes of buffalo mozzarella and fresh
mozzarella and margherita pizza and Camogliese pizza and
puffed rice folded into chocolate honey rum and candied
fruit and hazelnuts and almonds to make chewy torrone and
rice pilaf and soufflé of onions potatoes tomatoes peppers
and roasted eggplant and spaghetti with clams and carbonara
with egg prosciutto and pancetta and bread with butter and
sugar and bread with garlic oil and tomato and cocoa-dusted
ricotta and Valtellina pizzoccheri blanched with potatoes

spinach chard and dressed with butter oil parmesan sage thyme and bay leaf and cheese pies and crepes with marmalade and frittatas with vegetables with cheese and basil and pies with artichokes peas cabbage and potatoes baked in shortcrust and glorious Caprese cakes with almonds and rum and chocolate I will sit at the feet of the celestial thrones and offer the angels and demons and God Santa Rosa sfogliatelle and cannoli fried sheep brain and veal and artichokes and cabbage and golden-fried zucchini and trays of steamed artichokes with garlic and parsley and oil in their tender hearts and golden-fried artichokes and golden-fried zucchini and eggplant and roasted eggplant stuffed with pasta and meat and roasted eggplant stuffed with old bread mixed with water capers tomatoes cubes of mozzarella and parmesan until the breadcrumb surface turns golden and pieces of buffalo mozzarella in their glorious milk and rapini and rabe and rice balls with meat and ragù and peas and potato croquettes and shortbread cookies and beignets stuffed with meat and with pastry cream and the glory that is the Neapolitan pastiera with orange blossom-infused ricotta and cassata with pistachio and almond paste glaze candied fruit and ricotta and thousands upon thousands of trays filled with cakes made with layers of cream and glaze and chocolate and thousandfold millefoglie made by alternating layers of thin sheet pastry with layers of cream with butter and cream and powdered sugar and chocolate torrone made by pouring into molds chocolate almonds hazelnuts and whipped egg and pumpkin pasta and tagliolini in broth and in sauce and pappardelle and ravioli with walnut sauce and trofie with Ligurian pesto creamed with milk and meat ravioli and pumpkin ravioli and ravioli with cheese and ricotta and meat tagliolini in broth and spinach-ricotta ravioli in sage and butter and potato prosciutto mozzarella and cheese gateaux and thousands upon thousands of breaded mozzarellas and sautéed rabe and escarole pies made by stuffing trays of dough made with lightly sautéed escarole with pine nuts and raisins and a dash of salt and baked on low until golden brown and beef stew made by putting in cold water celery onion potato with shank bone and fat shoulder meat a piece of stew beef and all the spices thyme sage oregano parsley capers basil which are the glory of the Mediterranean garden and little plates of Brussels sprouts and cabbage dressed with ribbons of anchovy and sardines and parsley oil basil and green and black Gaeta olives and fried marinated anchovies and fried mozzarella and fresh mozzarella garnished with San Marzano tomatoes with garlic basil and oil and bread with butter and jam and bread with butter and sugar and bread with butter and tuna and cups of milk and cookies and malt and hard friselle softened in water and topped with diced fresh tomato and basil and oil and salt and mozzarella and fiordilatte and sugary fried doughnuts and buttery pastries and purees of meat and flour and vegetables or broth and fish I made for my daughter when she was a baby and little pastries made in the shape of little breasts or horns or golden hills and almond cookies and pasta casseroles and turkeys with sausage-chestnut stuffing and other meats and ricotta and peas This will be my glory that I lay at the feet of God and the feet of my living and my dead I will cover the cosmos-sheet where life is frescoed with the pleasures of the belly I will lay at the feet of God my solitary and eternal domesticitude in my kitchen somewhere under the Po Lowland skies This has been my talent My God Love me God Love me for all eternity I have scattered the flavors and scents of my cooking across the world

Accept my gift—Reader—I have fought my battle in life with food I've erected to the heavens cathedrals of pastry and baked longing and pleasure Accept my gift—Reader—I am only a woman I sleep alone

As my mind kept drifting back to the gun my eyes shifted back to my daughter's hands and the little hands of the beautiful woman all alone In the dining room the fires of heaven and hell blazed The host of demons and angels sang and in the chaos where matter materializes nature naturalizes things thingify and God godifies I served the meat pies and cream-filled zeppole dropping with dark cherry blood in the pubis of cream

A trickle of cherry blood ran down the beautiful lone woman's little lips They were curved in a smile of cream and longing that made the blood race through her veins where a demon was murmuring And it was the God of the body unleashing the madness in her soul as a woman alone I wanted to know everything about her I wanted to enter into her mystique I didn't want to possess her or conquer her I didn't want to inflict violence on anyone Her husband looked at her with concupiscent eyes lazy with desire He lavished her with longing furs and jewels and chokers Her mild frustration loosened in her chest and her eyes As a young woman she had made a marriage of convenience to offset the death that befell her family house after the death of her rich industrialist entrepreneur father from Romagna transplanted to the Po Lowlands with his entire family of five children a wife and relatives all living in the same house The funeral was on a rainy Christmas day They all went to the cemetery on a hill in the Romagnan countryside with a view of the distant Adriatic shores of Cattolica where Botero's fat women fat housebound hens wash dishes in winter and in summer fatten up like obscene pigs with little blond piglet children A tourism of office workers and wage slaves hanging off the magnificent winter towers of lifeguards in striped costumes on deserted beaches populated by the infinitude of a thousand cabanas and identical blue-and-white-striped umbrellas like the tired pale color high in the Romagnan sky vast over the infinite sands The Adriatic coast is a gold mine of lost things And the fat Botero women rest languidly on their longed-for and their lost loves Eyes lost in the vacuity of industrial unease Older mothers pecked at heaping plates of pasta counting the slow rosary of the days their laden bellies swollen with aches and laments Perhaps for their faraway children Young mothers big fat flabby and vulgar clucked like happy hens in a henhouse Blue and orange mixed with pink were the shades of the local kitsch Cheap tacky shell souvenirs were displayed in streetside shops In Romagna fat men lean on the tired yet firm absolute and glorious plenitude of a metaphysical landscape like an empty fascist Italian piazza And the fat Tuscan hens pecked same as the Romagnan and the Neapolitan in the most beautiful gardens of Italy At the thought of their young the Neapolitan women bourgeois peasant proletariat servant housewives and wives to postal workers and rail employees felt their motherly blood boil in their veins Looking at the Cézannean bathers teenage sweethearts and rebel nuns the Neapolitan mothers felt the carnivalesque spirit of their lost childhoods embodied in the thousands of fat children crowding the magnificent long metaphysical beaches of Italy

And I looked at the others We were surrounded by onlookers and we dropped everything that was weighing us down leaving us uneasy and tormented We ran into the mad summer rush before us with the long-reaching shadows of the sublime Italian landscape Then the onlookers fell to the ground in the dust of time And time became a hallucinatory return between bags sandwiches suitcases and humans of all ages packed into a train station in a suffocating heat Outside the train windows among smells of bananas and salami sandwiches the great slow Italian landscape slowly rolled past

Everyone was bored Except a current of melancholy and sorrow crossed the tired lips of the middle-class doctors and entrepreneurs and industrialists and office workers who had come in procession to pay respects to an illustrious and devout corpse The man had always donated money and contributed to the humanitarian associations that lined up at his door asking for cash and aid for the wars that plague this earth The beautiful woman's mother dressed in black and longing spoke sorrowful and slow She addressed the crowd and said "My husband was worthy of respect He was a philanthropist He did good things for everyone That's why as you know our food business was headed for ruin Sausages salamis fresh and aged cheese canned tuna ox meat ox quarters chicken frozen foods and jams and preserves and sugar and rice and rigatoni pennette ziti maltagliati maccheroni tagliolini tagliatelle risoni stelline rondelle yellow rice jasmine rice broken pasta to serve with chickpeas Everything was about to be devoured and consumed by worms and parasites of destruction Now go with peaceful souls to say goodbye to a man of honor" The crowd knew the wealthy industrialist in the food business used philanthropy to cover up his power He wanted to be father and master to all but he miscalculated His greed turned against him He'd had mistresses His wife knew it the beautiful woman knew it too

The hangers-on that appear when a person of wealth dies dispersed The five children gathered at the house The beautiful woman was the only one who could reverse the fortunes of a ruined family Her brothers and sisters were inept at commerce business and trade and they were still young Without mincing words her mother said "My girl you must marry a rich man who will let you take the reins of the family business" The beautiful woman agreed that she wouldn't oppose a match She wasn't interested in men She just liked the comfortable life the clothes the food the jewelry At the post-funeral reception she wolfed down the baked pasta made by their last remaining servant And now at my trattoria the teeth in her rosebud mouth sank into the meat pies and the stews the zeppole the Caprese and the cabbage salad dressed with anchovies parsley oil olives and mayonnaise The dark cherry blood of the jam from the pubis of golden-blond pastry dripped on her chest A rivulet of wine trickled between her breasts My cooking was so strange and wild compared to what she knew at home where the chef was just a servant without the wisdom of food in his manly hands Her mother had proposed different suitors for her daughter They were discussed in the same way as a shopping list since they knew that beauty is a key that can open any door They decided on a food entrepreneur like her father: a fat little Botero man who spent his life among ham hocks cheese wheels cold cuts sausages sugar jam broccoli potatoes cod mullet scorpionfish octopus sturgeon salmon tuna hake swordfish sole flatfish and frozen food fried food snack cakes torrone chocolate candies flour and breads of all shapes and sizes butter and yogurt and pudding Olivier salad tortelli ravioli soft cheese ice cream fish sticks and meat and pizza and vegetables fruit and water and wines and liqueurs in every size of bottle He was a fat and eminently respectable marriageable entrepreneur A dinner was arranged with the mother children and relatives from the neighborhood who sat around the table at a restaurant in which the entrepreneur had stock They sat and devoured pasta e ceci made with broken tagliatelle in chickpea puree with butter rosemary sage garlic oil milk and ricotta Then they demolished a meatloaf filled with peas egg ricotta in a golden crust with a side of salad and boiled potatoes and roasted potatoes They ate without shame There was no talk of marriage There reigned only the strident silence of God of the food on the table lavished with manna from God who sings in the chaos in which things thingify matter materializes nature naturalizes creation is created And God godifies He eyed the beautiful woman's bosom Her mother said in no uncertain terms "This marriage has to happen As you know yesterday was my husband's funeral If we come together we can create the biggest food company in all of southern Padania" His greedy and crafty eyes could already see the warehouses in southern Padania with a constant stream of trucks and vans transporting preserves and meats and products of every sort and size

As I watched the beautiful woman and read her story in the cards of the sky she flashed me an amorous look woman to woman I placed my hand on hers under the eyes of her husband who looked the other way at any promiscuity I reached out to cut thin slices of Caprese cake and serve the zeppole with the pubis bleeding cream and cherry Tina looked at me from the remote distance of her better years The dark floral dress she was wearing for me fell over the wide round hips of a woman broken by toil As payback for my touching the beautiful woman she went in the kitchen and turned on her infernal vacuum whose thunderous rumble contaminated the aromatic air of roast and soup and sweets and orange blossoms inside Da Rosa

I looked at the wide hips of the lone little woman You could see she wasn't happy with an older husband The dissatisfaction of an unwanted marriage was written on her face But she buried all her bitterness with food I decided that I would take her out the next day when the restaurant would be closed That night I served cream and chocolate beignets made with a dense cream filling of butter cocoa sugar and milk simmered on low heat until the mixture thickened My patrons scattered slow into the night The fires of the orgy that had filled the Da Rosa dining room with debauchery rose toward the sky and the tall ramparts of the world The big Botero women's shawls slid down broad shoulders where their earrings and necklaces dangled They leaned on the arms of their husbands who supported them drunk on wine and liqueurs In the low-slung skies of Padania the angelic and infernal hosts sang I sleep alone— Reader—I am a woman alone I know how to use my talents to rouse desire and pleasure even in spent souls like those of my patrons devoted to nothing but commerce and trade I watched them stumble toward their everyday fates

3

I saw my patrons thronging in the Po Lowland landscape of longing The big Botero women buttoned coats and jackets and vanished into the fog of canals docks poplars maples and birches of the soft Lombard landscape where I'd grown used to living with my daughter after leaving Naples Same as Tina I lacked a man She said to me "I'm jealous of that beautiful woman" I looked at the rich Romagnan industrialist's wife bored by the wealth that had driven her to an idle life of mere consumption leaving her like Oblomov sprawled out on the divan in her bedroom She let the dust settle on her She lay there eating bonbons for days Dust coated everything around her the undisputed mistress of all things Combs perfumes creams oils books cushions blankets sheets vanity and stool were enveloped in volutes of dust the fumes of the eternal dust in which matter materializes nature naturalizes things thingify and God godifies In the dust things became themselves in her uncontested domain where the great book of memory is read and written Lifting her little hand to her belly and her mouth she looked out at the flat Padan landscape irrigated with fountains canals and industrial pumps Now and then the husband appeared and she made room for him in the bed Bored and acquiescent she accepted him in her arms And now, in the kitchen, thinking of that contact of her as my new womanly love I felt a twinge in my spine of iron and dead children's bones The beautiful woman like all women—Reader—had a spine of iron and dead children's bones in her ravaged womanly flesh Her husband's hands snaked sneakily beneath the sheets Ardent and indiscreet they probed her She knew she had to appease him She let herself be touched without shame She had never taken an interest in the lot of the marital business Sex was just the means to secure her font of riches Their sweaty bodies united He turned her over pressing his mouth to her breast and her pubis He ravaged her with his big imperious male hands like a vizier who kept her enchained with his money

The next day after having cleared the kitchen of the previous night's great feast when the celestial and infernal powers danced inside my restaurant of which I say with pride "This is mine, this is the fruit of my labor as a woman alone who knows she is the mistress of her own destiny" but that now was getting lost in the frenzy of my lesbian love So I would have enough time to go visit the beautiful woman I began the next day's cooking with a potato casserole and broccoli pasta and artichokes and peas and carrots mixed with ricotta béchamel milk and mozzarella arranged over pastry crust with criss-cross strips on top like a crostata I made three trays and six others of casserole and sliced very thin cutlets of veal and roast beef and arranged them on white porcelain serving platters painted with blue Chinese pagodas and reeds and streams and peasants lost in the boundless white and blue of an imaginary China I smothered the cutlets with tuna sauce mixed with capers anchovies green and black Gaeta olives parsley oil and a dash of vinegar I wreathed the meat with boiled potatoes garnished with radishes anchovies lettuce arugula olives and cauliflower and mandolined zucchini and julienned carrot I put it all in the fridge along with the sausages I had covered with a crown of crust which looked like Achilles' shield surrounded by the Okeanos River I recalled in *The Odyssey* the two deadly warriors and Achilles' deadly wrath which brought the Achaeans so much suffering It was a metaphysical wrath that offered up to the heavens the story of the destruction of Troy The great mother of Hector and Hecuba and Paris who out of love for a beautiful woman unleashed the wrath of Agamemnon and the gods of the earth and the sky and the sea pitting Poseidon against Odysseus the first wandering Jew in the history of the West who belongs to this sea finite flayed furrowed by ships carrying centuries gold millennia wines spices oils handicrafts freemen slaves This sea struck by waves by lights which never forgets a vessel a lighthouse a house This sea of buried dead And back come the millennia and centuries past the buried and reanimated dead and dark women hunched shrunken They weave cloth by the sea They wait rip stitch add rip hook gather They give substance to the sea A sea written drawn corporeal They make it the open closed body of the age-old sea barred with columns with vessels with lighthouses Sea of war sea of earth paper sea of flesh paper Egyptian Sicilian African sea Italian sea Sea of Spain France Greece Albania Roman sea inked handcrafted articulated sea fatigued never tired of setting forth Mediterranean

After tidying up I put on a clean black dress Everything was all ready for the next day I headed toward Monticelli I knew where she lived It was the nicest house around It was an old farmhouse whose granaries had been repurposed as warehouses for the family business The house was three stories with walls as high and strong as the tall ramparts of the sky Ivy and creeping vines twisted up the walls of the house-fortress as they did up the high walls of the world Farmers with hoes and rakes and tractors and bulldozers full of hay tended to their animals in the stables Oxen horses rabbits goats sheep grazed freely in the yard which was as big as a place-of-arms

The animals bleated and brayed amid the chirping of cicadas crickets flies and mosquitoes that brought to mind the expanse of olive trees in whose infinitude my childhood play unfolded and where my childhood still lies buried marked by a wooden cross buried along with the gun of my childhood which I replaced with the gun I keep in my bedside drawer which only my cooking and the ancient knowledge of my hands and my love for all women keep me away from I looked at the house feeling lost I felt like soft dough in an infinite vortex consuming its own substance I heard the universe and the planets colliding with a precipitous screech of splitting rock of bloody swords of crust shifting of pavement and then softening to the point of destruction its fragmented matter disintegrated molecules churning

If one day the planets fell and the mysterious strings that keep them painfully bound to the sky slackened and wavered uncertain like swings abandoned by their occupants who clutched the ropes and searched each other's eyes in hesitation before taking the leap

If the compact mass were to yield revealing its true precarious nature the uncertain calculation keeping it intact

If like wounded doves the planets fell into the immense into the infinite tunnel that separates us all and immense boundless grinds and grinds

With the world fallen and resurrected once again I saw the tall ramparts of my beautiful lady's house collapse and resurge I already imagined so many things about her I caught sight of her in the third-floor window her face tense and pale Walking slow and soft I headed toward her house passing through the commerce taking place in the yard where trucks were pulling up with frozen meat to be stored in her husband's company's walk-in coolers He negotiated with the steward and the workers he had trained to keep her free from work The moment they married he realized she wasn't cut out for labor just to be mounted and ravaged in bed and in this way honoring the deal the family had made with that union of convenience She wore white on their wedding day Her tiny waist was cinched with a wide silk sash with a satin rose The dress embroidered with roses and wisteria and anemones and butterflies and spiders hugged her sumptuous matronly breasts and hips Slender pointed-toe slippers peeped out from the gown's long hem and made her hobble like a little Chinese woman in tight clogs shuffling down a gravel path Her velvety cheeks rosy with blush she was the portrait of the opulence of the industrial bourgeoisie of the Po Lowlands He too was big and fat squeezed into a gray satin vest under a gray-and-white raw linen pinstripe suit that pulled at his sides his crotch and his joints He had a thin oiled mustache that glistened on his pale face and highlighted his thin mouth taut with longing and lust for power Theirs was a lavish and ornate ceremony brightened by the tossing of the white rose and pink orchid bouquet promising its recipient imminent marriage They had a luncheon banquet with many dishes All the guests possessed with orgiastic fervor and wine and drink had devoured timbales of tagliolini with ragù and meatballs and peas and mozzarella and sliced artichoke and prosciutto and scampi cocktails with salmon sauce and lemon and meat with tartar sauce and sausage and roasted chicken There was a seventeenth-century-style pasta cathedral composed of three tiers with savory cannoli and a golden crust over meat meatballs ricotta and ziti in the shape of a cathedral with its doughy dome egg coated and baked until golden The poor were kept out of church and wealthy homes creating a habitual contrast in the affluent context of Padania where the poor had become scarce and were often just rebellious intellectuals or workers who'd been laid off when the global market fell The food entrepreneurs and industrialists took care not to upset their laborers and lower-class workers to avoid creating the conditions for civil or political unrest

As the guests dispersed in the late afternoon the Botero bride received kisses from her ambivalent mother and her brothers who were satisfied with the transaction They all knew there was no love in it Everyone played their part And the most difficult belonged to my beautiful lady who was in for a fate of dissatisfaction and boredom I watched her walk amid the sounds of animals and laborers across the extravagant farmyard which had retained a rustic feel On that late spring morning in the Po Lowlands I knocked at the door I smoothed my black dress over my hips I fixed my hair I was greeted by a uniformed housemaid like a servant at an elegant manor But the beautiful woman didn't require elegance She had succumbed to neglect She didn't even ask for her bedroom to be dusted As a woman I aroused no suspicion of infidelity when I asked to see the lady of the house I was told to wait She showed me upstairs and I asked for a coffee

They all knew who I was: the proprietor and chef of the restaurant Da Rosa which every night drew throngs of people from Padania Brianza Piedmont Tuscany Romagna reawakening the craving for pleasure in the little town of Monticelli They were all enticed by my renowned enterprise where I utilized the age-old knowledge of food and hands passed down to me from my mother The housekeeper came down and said that the lady of the house was ready for me As I awaited my coffee I lit a cigarette Her door swung open and she emerged wrapped in a clingy satin robe tied with a silk sash and a satin rose Her feet were shod in tiny marabou slippers that offered a peek of her slender ankles She had fine glossy black hair like a Russian doll She looked at me indolent and inquisitive She knew what I wanted We drank coffee in silence keeping up the appearance of polite and refined forms of courtesy Then knowingly and modestly I reached for her neck and her breasts I squeezed her little hand and planted a feathery light kiss on her lips which quivered on contact with the mouth of a woman who could have been her mother I told her I don't want to be your mother We'll be equals In a few days come with me to Chiaravalle and Morimondo and Crespi d'Adda I'll drive Our lips touched We stood at the window of her kingdom of trinkets chocolates and dust that fell on the disused things feelings people It was the opulent and hollow life of a woman alone I told her tenderly "I'll always be there for you" I closed the door on the kingdom of dust which loomed quiet over everything The room was dimly lit I didn't want to lock the stars away in a tower I didn't want to dominate I didn't want to trap stars between the walls of heaven I looked at her in the closed dimly lit room where the stars cast bands of light that refracted on the cosmos-sheet where life is frescoed Her soft breasts were an offering of love to the angels and demons of heaven I didn't want to lock the stars away in a tower Life is an endless cavalcade through heaven's eternal meadows and the demonic underworld: all through our lives we carry our baggage of flesh and objects papers thoughts I didn't want to lock the sky and the stars away in a tower in the dust of the cosmos and sky In the dimly lit room dust fell on the sheer lampshade that seemed to be made of women's skin like something a Nazi officer in the Second World War divided between a sense of duty and horror of the camps would have had on his desk where he kept a gun He knew what the lampshade was made of He knew he was washing himself with the same soap made from human fat that he used to shine his shoes I talked to the beautiful woman in her room over the farmyard bustling with traffic and trade where workers went back and forth seeing to the animals distributing goods and taking hoes tractors rakes out to the fields in a glorious rapture of voices and noise I told her the story about the Nazi officer and his lamp Her little hand reached toward her nightstand and touched the lamp I took her hand and said "In three days let's go on a little trip I'll come and take you away" She looked at me hesitantly She could feel the crack of her husband's whip at her back She was a transgressive woman whose transgression was made of laxity and abandon She would've been blown over by the slightest puff of wind She was as changeable as the ribbon on her hat and the iridescent glints of the roses on her robes and clothes She was a flower of a woman grown in a garden of omnivorous plants She went on downing bonbons and coffee I told her that for that night at the restaurant I had prepared stews and timbales of pasta and sausage as well as a frittata with pasta and egg and rose made by blending butter ricotta fontina and ziti pan-fried with white lavender pink and black rose petals It was my gift to her I felt the flames of lust from the orgy that was about to recur at Da Rosa That night I had decided to limit the number of guests I wanted it calm I didn't want to lock the sky and the stars away in a tower We were still gazing out the window Holding my hand she said she would come with me We drank and ate pastries and chocolate Everything lay in a dust that seemed centuries-old Perfume bottles and paintings of portraits and gardens and still lifes were coated in that thin layer The dust of time In the semidarkness I stood up and smoothing my dress over my hips I emerged into the glorious rapture of sunlight My beautiful lady looked at me from the window of that house that represented the orgy of power Slowly the tractors lined up in the sun-swathed countryside full of blond fields of grain that stood tall with their needly stalks pointing up toward the vault of heaven surrounded by rows of rhododendrons hawthorn and meadows of poppies and daisies and fields of corn with blond and brown silk In the sun the water shimmered in rivers and canals metal tubes that fanned out like arteries and veins from the heart of the Po Lowlands Slowly I returned home in the soon-setting sun I lay down in bed I undressed soft and slow I slipped off my clothes and slid under my sheets of longing where I shared with myself the pleasure of existing Soft and slow I touched myself until I heard my daughter come upstairs and go into her room I felt happy apprehensive and eager but I didn't want to lock the sky and stars away in a tower After an hour I got up I put on a black dress that contained my fatter form In the kitchen I drank wine and snacked on chips and olives I sat at the table with my neighbor and daughter and we ate a small timbale of ziti au gratin I had made just for us The soft sauce pooled at the edges of our mouths like rivulets of blood running from the lips of sirens who devour the bones of errant men After dinner we ate zeppole with absinthe and wine Then I ordered the bones of creation in the drawers Up high bones and stardust At the very top the bones of God On the left the bones of the heart Overhead of the living and of the dead And inside the cabinet the bones of the bodies of the ancestors In the liver the bones of my mother and my father and my dead brother I maintained the bones of creation I kept them dusted You shouldn't be dirty when you're dead Death comes soft and gentle devouring the dust of time grinding bones marrow sperm eggs liver brain soul stardust Death when it comes the earth quakes Death when it comes bends stars constellations and galaxies to its will Death when it comes the universe falls silent in a sign of utmost respect for

the evanescence of a mere mosquito or midge The seas quake
the earth quakes The angels and demons of God quake Up
rises the catastrophe of a tremendous seaquake that throttles
the shores of an entire life

After eating the zeppole I saw my fatter figure in the mirror
It would help me win over the beautiful woman whom I saw far
away lying in her bed of dust and longing I could feel her flesh
in my hand with her spoiled girlish soul I recalled the dust in
that musty room in the richest house in town I was swept away
senses and mind by my latest lady love For an instant the gun
in the nightstand drawer flashed in my mind I wouldn't use it
I didn't want to lock the stars away in a tower Stars should be
kept free from ties bonds chains The cosmos chaos constellations galaxies head toward their destiny unfettered pulling
along in the void of everything the cosmos-sheet where life is
frescoed

My lips still stained with sauce and cream I made the rounds
in the kitchen I turned on the oven and stove Timbales and
casseroles sizzled in the heat of the oven that reddened our
round cheeks I put to roast over the coals a small goose stuffed
with chestnuts meatballs pancetta old bread mixed with ricotta
and cheese and prosciutto I tied it with twine and placed it on
a delicate Chinese porcelain platter surrounded by sprigs of
fennel and roasted potatoes and brussels sprouts and rose-cut
radishes and julienned carrots At eight p.m. that evening's
small group of guests flocked from their houses They were
the richest in Monticelli the most hedonistic and wanton
advancing down the roads of life and climbing the ladders of
heaven the way the circles of hell buckled under the weight
of Sisyphus's boulder Every day like a burden they bore the
endeavor of their industry and their life on their shoulders
I watched them devour the timbales of pasta the tortellini in

broth filled with mince mixed with prosciutto ricotta parmesan pancetta They were the revelers of the circles of hell

Now and then I thought about my beautiful lady and our trip and I recalled the strident thunderous roar of the vacuum with its madness of time and clocks Everyone ate devouring in silence Chests heaved with warm groans of delight Nostrils fluttered taking in the scents of casseroles and roasts I felt the fecund ancient wisdom in my hands passed down from my mother The room buzzed with an unspoken and subtle frisson It was a greater sensual pleasure than with the crowded and raucous bacchanal I served the cassata the zeppole and the beignets that I had made that morning They were doused in the silver-gold fire of Spanish wine and cognac and grappa and vodka Outside the ground froze under the thin layer of frost that covered the countryside and the silent plowed fields in whose cold arms the fire of the sensual pleasure of food stoked at Da Rosa emerged in the low Lombard sky And I saw my ship sailing with the name Rosa printed on its side That was my name I gave it to myself I didn't want to lock my life the sky the stars away in a tower

It was one a.m. The crowd dispersed in their black clothes over their skin flush from the heat and the food and the fire in the silent cold of the frost-shimmering countryside of the Po Lowlands My daughter neighbor and I cleaned the room Tina back home fired up her infernal vacuum I climbed into bed next to my daughter who that night had wanted to sleep with me like a little girl I could feel in the night the frenzied rumble of the vacuum of the demons and of God a God of bodies that rose high over all things of the world of death and of life that paraded through the windless night We closed our eyes till the next morning Only two more days till my little trip I didn't want to lock the sky the stars my life away in a tower

I wanted to see my beautiful lady happy smiling away from the infernal circles of a rich monotonous life I spent two identical gray days making timbales of pasta and bean soups made by combining golden Italian rice with chickpeas and lentils with ricotta rosemary sage a little milk and oil I prepared a separate dish of Neapolitan fagioli della regina mixing white rice with borlotti slow-cooked in diced fresh tomato garlic oil and a splash of milk then I made thin cutlets of veal coated in flour and lemon butter wine sage and rosemary and steamed potatoes from Romagna and an Olivier salad made with cubes of potato carrot beet peas cabbage and capers with mayonnaise and tuna sauce Then I made a big potato-fish by molding a mixture of tuna potatoes ricotta and mayonnaise with cubes of steamed swordfish and boiled shrimp garnished with radish and carrot and little rosebuds and daisies and capers and green and black Gaeta olives and parsley and sliced lemon and quartered orange and rosettes of mayonnaise and ricotta It was a sophisticated dish that I enhanced by adding a little rum to the mayonnaise The fish was like a ship sailing the ancient surface of the seas toward its destiny of pleasure

After a calmer night the next two brought us a multitude of guests They paced and paused at the tables unconscious of themselves and of life The ancient knowledge in my hands led them to the luxury of mindlessness bliss and oblivion They let go of their daily cares The night dispelled the same monotony I had also felt in the kitchen after my lady's departure Now I was proud of my art confident I could resurrect souls and bodies with the luxuriance of food I watched them eat with a greater sense of solidarity and sympathy The constancy of pleasure dampened fires too violent to bear every night of our life And in the quiet dust of time I saw my food slowly entering satiating bodies and souls with pleasure I was gratified by the beautiful shapes I'd given my fish and timbales I was glad to see the little cathedrals of pasta en croute Everything entered the hungry bodies without traces without leftovers without waste without pain without excess on this umpteenth night of pleasure Perhaps the violent bacchanals would recur but I knew I was soon to take a break with my beautiful lady They washed down the food with wine and liqueur Their cheeks flushed Their eyes gleamed in a restrained tranquility with hints of latent fire

After two days of work I went back to see her Traffic and trade and work went on in the yard The steward was haggling with a local businessman who wanted to buy quarters of ox of beef of veal of lamb for his supermarket but the steward knew to concede nothing to the competition He said that the stock wasn't for sale "Your boss is a real taskmaster" the visitor said "Yes" the steward said "he knows what he's doing even in the mess of small industrial and agricultural business" You could hear the rumble of the threshers mowing the grain and the excavators that gathered and deposited bales of hay in the barns as if constructing the ramparts of a fortress amid the boisterous voices of men women and children In that rustic landscape which seemed more cheerful that morning I turned my gaze toward her window It was shielded by heavy shutters I imagined her half-undressed lying on the bed or the dusty divan in her room in that space of dust and perfume where her life evaporated like water in an aquarium Perhaps that woman who had only her servitude as a wealthy lady mistress of nothing but her dissatisfaction and boredom thought about me I didn't want to lock her life and mine and the sky and the stars and God away in a tower Maybe she had forgotten our date It was after all a kind of betrayal

It was almost Easter The children of the farmers and laborers played in the yard carrying twigs from the olive tree and clutching big chocolate eggs they would open on the day of the resurrection of the dead when the earth would tremble and trigger a violent seaquake from whose depths an anomalous wave would surge and slam into the land frenetic with quaking and the seven seals of the horsemen of the apocalypse would open Life's end coincides with every Easter every hour every day with dawn when the dead rise from their graves God doesn't want to lock humans and God and earth and the planets and the constellations and the sun and the cosmos away in a tower God makes his creations free to take part in the cosmos in which matter materializes nature naturalizes things thingify And God godifies in the initial and final catastrophe of the resurrection which at every instant and every day of death and life takes place and is repeated

An oleograph of youth formed in the yard with the jocular children and industrious farmhands in a sugary pink April landscape behind which I saw the truth of the blood and flesh of an immolated God with all of humanity on the cross of an eternal calvary It was a bloody April that reminded me in its pomp and pleasure that I sleep alone When I die I'll bring my living and my dead all the struffoli and crostatas and beignets and savory pies and fried pizzelle that I learned from my mother's age-old art

My lady's window parted and her petite form appeared and disappeared in the closed-in shadows of her room a prison of dust bonbons and perfume As a present I'd brought her some chocolates I'd made by melting chocolate with rum and coffee with sprinkles and hearts of pistachio almond walnut hazelnut and soft truffles made by mixing crumbled cookies and cocoa and coffee with rum and egg dusted with powdered sugar and coffee powder I went to have myself announced I asked for coffee liqueur and wine I found her languidly outstretched on the dusty divan in her room of hebetude and boredom with the unquiet dust on her young shoulders I watched her with pleasure and pain I realized that even in this new love I slept alone I offered her the chocolates She unwrapped the package full of delights and strong scents Her little pearl teeth sank into the nearly pitch-black chestnut hearts We leisurely sipped coffee and liqueurs and ate chocolates I held her hand silent in mine I reminded her of the trip She had nearly forgotten She went to get ready For an instant I felt betrayed but I didn't want to lock the sky the stars God and our lives away in a tower

Languidly she arose from the divan and packed a leather and satin valise with silk pajamas a leather train case a mother-of-pearl brush with animal bristles and satin marabou slippers She stole away to the bathroom I heard the water pouring in the tub Slowly I opened the door and I saw her curvaceous pale and delicate body descend into the water as if into an aquarium of fish and mermaids She scrubbed her skin carefully with lazy hands She had added oils and perfumes that emanated from the bath's thick steam I saw her as a fetus in a pearly white womb of water She was as far away as a mermaid in a fairy tale Even in love we are each of us alone—Reader—The scale of my passion was diminishing Maybe it was just a little adventure but I still wanted to enjoy it and interrupt the frenetic pace of the feasts and work with easy pleasure

When she was ready in her wool and silk dress we went down without raising suspicion She phoned her husband to tell him she was going out with a friend I was grateful to her for not saying my name We got in the car and headed to Vigevano where I was taking her to a warm and inviting restaurant I knew From the car we saw rows of canals granaries farms and fountains in that bloody April sun The Ticino carved through the low landscape of the Padan Plain like a watery sword tired and still after having raged and swirled It was a peaceful and grand sight in the Lombard mists We reached Vigevano with its massive place-of-arms along the walls of the Renaissance castle with its tower overlooking the seventeenth-century palace surrounding the square which was one of the most beautiful in Italy We headed toward the big clearing outside the castle We parked the car and visited the royal stables where a long Renaissance colonnade once held horses We could see them in our mind's eye nostrils flaring and knights astride The castle was closed to visitors We went to the restaurant I knew and chickens were roasting on the fire They poured us red wine I saw my big Botero woman's little lips pearled with droplets of wine and sweat We ate baked pasta made with béchamel peas prosciutto cheese and mozzarella The milky sauce slid into our mouths hungry with longing

After the baked pasta we dug into a Gallura hen whose little bones tickled our palates and throats My spine of iron and dead children's bones ached I looked at her and her wide womanly hips We drank Lacryma Christi which glided down our throats reawakening ancient desires There were few diners around us Night was falling We emerged onto the beautiful ovaline piazza We strolled by the market stands selling grains dates figs almonds chickpeas lentils white beans black beans green peas black peas Some of the stands sold empty shoes that reminded me of Tina Empty shoes evoke the plenitude of their future wearer

We headed to the pensione where we asked for a single room We lay down the entire long afternoon with the shadows of evening starting to fall The room had a bed with a red damask cover with embroidered silk flowers and reproductions of gardens and flowers on the walls We uncovered the freshly cleaned white pillows She undressed soft and slow We decided to give in to the languor and sensual pleasure of bed rather than go out at least for the first day of our trip We ordered wine coffee and chocolates to our room We set the tray of honey and zuccherini and shortbread on the bed as we caressed each other eating and drinking

I squeezed her open Her pubis with its rosy perfume parted in my hand like a flower in bloom like a carnivorous plant that devours all the others that cross its path Our hands searched each other light sticky like a shroud of cocoa sugar and liqueur I placed zuccherini on the tip of her tongue delighted to see that delicate organ take on the colors of the powdered sugar blue lilac violet cyan green Water colors that suited her lonely sirenic life She was beautiful in her nakedness that had been violated by a commanding power-hungry man's hands We joined our lips in a latch of love charged with want Our legs intertwined like tentacular sea creatures under the lunar cosmos-sheet where life is frescoed I swirled wine and spices in her glass I wanted to stun her with scents and spirits She held me languid and light like a siren who contains the fathoms of a sea made of traffic trade industry farmers and laborers and stewards and men and women and children She let me cradle her in my arms to the slow and solemn deep music of desire and longing Her little feet peeked out soft and slow from the blood-red satin enclosing her like a pelt of blood And it was the late spring of a bloody April that conjoined water and earth in a sea of desire and longing that transformed my motherly womb and that of mother earth into that of a vestal virgin guardian of time Like a terrifying growl I could hear the infernal call of Tina's vacuum cleaner that dominated the cosmos-sheet where life is frescoed The vacuum's infernal song destroyed the harmony of chaos in which matter materializes nature naturalizes things thingify and God godifies I ran my mature woman's hand back and forth from bosom to pubis from tiptoe to fingertip I penetrated her slow and soft with my fingers which were consumed from the labor of cleaning and cooking which contains the ancient wisdom of food On the tip of her tongue I placed chocolate squares and flakes and powdered sugar that slid soft down her beautiful womanly throat I ran my hands over her skin from the hillocks of her breasts to the promontories of her hips which rose from her little woman's body spoiled by life After hours of lovemaking I covered her with the blood-red brocade I closed my lids over my tired eyes She still held my hand in hers I looked at her the way a mother looks at her creature made of scales fins and wants The world around me seemed to swirl as if currents of energy filled the calm wind where our love dissipated I saw behind her the shadow of her life and shepherds and farmers and fields and barns and traffic and trade and power and industry and stewards and bridges and roads and farmyards and sprinkles and perfumes and furs and bonbons and jewels covered with the disquiet dust of time that asks only to be freed from the snares of greed and insatiable Western hunger She was a creature of fire and passion restrained in the stagnation of a closed-up dust-covered room away from the world and its cries A cloistered nun's cell Her lone woman's life was barricaded behind heavy curtains of iron and dead children's bones

At nine p.m. I woke up while in the sky the deciduous queens of night reigned over heaven and earth I didn't want to lock her life and mine and the sky and the stars and God away in a tower She had gotten up when it was nearly night We went to the bathroom to freshen up I scrubbed her back under the dripping shower She scrubbed mine We smoothed each other like a couple of fish in an aquarium of white and fleeting and cerulean steam I told her "I will always be there for you I'll never leave you alone in your lone woman's hell" She looked at me without speaking I squeezed her breasts in my hands We dressed in turn squeezing ourselves into skirts and bras We went down to the dining room dressed in black traversed by flashes of the incipient night illuminated by pale moonbeams Her face bore the signs of requited love We sat at the table to eat shrimp and crispy rice balls with chicken and seafood washed down with Lacryma Christi which ran down our throats parched from the intense afternoon love I watched each bite disappear into her rosebud mouth The side room of the restaurant illuminated by blue flashes of brocade was nearly empty There was only one woman alone like the lone woman in the Hopper painting sitting by herself at a bar She was pale as a Greek kore and looked around darkly and ate stiffly I liked her I love all women I sleep alone

The beautiful little woman ate with gusto the tagliolini with cream butter sage and baby shrimp from Spain they'd served us on white-blue porcelain plates adorning each presentation with sprigs of parsley and basil and thyme and mayonnaise It was an enclosure of desires that rose in our eyes and our senses fecund with wanting I watched her devour the tagliolini that dripped with sauce and pleasures of the belly My beautiful lady knew how to find pleasure in her life They brought us Gallura cockerel accompanied by roasted potatoes and salad with mayonnaise and anchovies and green and black olives We washed down the food with fine wine She was from Gaeta a siren from the high seas Life—Reader—is an enclosure of longing in which you swim holding your breath in your throat drowning between feathers and scales At dinner they also served poached fish with ribbons of mayonnaise and soy sauce and sweet-and-sour pork and Cantonese duck and chicken in seaweed broth and delicate rose-scented lychees We drank lots of Lacryma Christi which dribbled from her little lips and pooled on her black silk dress at her groin spreading like a drop of blood over her sirenic body Looking at her again I knew that I slept alone

The wine stained the embroidered tablecloth like the ones I had inherited from my mother in her life as a woman alone watching me and my brother grow up We were raised in the endless expanse of olive trees blinded by the endless rays of sunshine in which matter materializes nature naturalizes things thingify and God godifies My mother passed down to me the madness of hands and cooking that I used in adding to my and her sweet cream and savory meat beignets a splash of rum which I had procured from the server at the pensione in Vigevano where we dined that first night of our trip After dinner we went out into that fat-mooned night in an April of blood that spread like a harbor of longing across Lombardy in the big oval space of the piazza protected and presided over by the tall Renaissance castle The stands with their empty shoes in their absolute metaphysical presence made me think of Tina and the rows of glittering fish and scorpionfish and octopus and seaweed and mullet and wedge clams and smooth clams and swordfish and tuna and stalls of cheap trinkets and of vegetables with cabbage with broccoli and Neapolitan rapini and broccoli rabe and radishes and salad and the flower stands with carnations in yellow white baby blue lavender red pink and anemones and daisies and orchids and wildflowers dog roses tulips gas plants irises columbines bellflowers Maltese crosses white lilies tiger lilies Loddon lilies Siberian irises peonies stock flowers pale narcissus jonquils Dalmatian irises marigolds wood lilies golden apple lilies paperwhite narcissus joss flowers love-in-a-mist daffodils Turk's cap lilies anemones peacock flowers cornflowers Dutch irises Dutch hyacinths Provence roses pink-white starflowers Roman chamomile common peonies lily leeks fringed pink narcissus lilacs Asian bleeding-heart jonquils Arabian starflowers Portuguese squill hyacinth squill lily-of-the-valley snowdrops grape hyacinths Alpine cyclamens African marigolds candytufts wild pansies winter daffodils autumn crocus Tahiti narcissus liverwort pennywort leatherflower globeflower wood anemone angel's trumpets marsh violet Neapolitan cyclamen forget-me-nots all closed up

The pale streetlight invaded and bathed the pitch-black pavement A light icy fog dampened our hair We walked arm in arm And it was one in the morning in a late bloody spring She shuffled in tiny steps like a geisha with her little Oriental feet I supported her soft and slow while my hands ordered the bones of creation: up on high the bones of the sky and of God Then down the bones of the dead children and the fathers and mothers of history On the right of the heart the bones of the angels and the demons and the horsemen of the apocalypse in the armor of their fate that leads them to exterminate the species before every resurrection which is repeated in the miracle of creation every day and night When we returned home after passing under a portico reflecting the light of a museum open at night shaded with ivy and verbena where we saw sculptures and paintings by Magritte Matisse and Miró like the ones I saw in Antibes years ago that were about to become the everyday landscape of my daughter's life Along the long corridors of the streets illuminated by twilight specters I offered her my hand I took her into the Pensione Certosa and to our room I undressed her soft and slow I rinsed the stained black satin dress The scent of perfume and food rose from her body She was dripping with heat love pleasure I kissed her arm I kissed her pubis and tasted her food again Again we tasted the chocolate and cream beignets and meat pies and the Gallura cockerel the taglioloni with butter sage rosemary milk butter cream and rum and the zeppole and the pastiera and the wine and we made meat of our flesh and food of our bodies We materialized the one to the other like a single piece of flesh a single material a single body a single being Our bodies fused into a carnal embrace like nothing we'd ever experienced Soul and mind became flesh of one flesh body of one body it was a moral transubstantiation of the soul and the material that enveloped our entire person And so food became the body and soul of our future days

I squeezed her soft in my arms as she purred like a cat in heat I couldn't impregnate her which meant our relationship was free of chains I ran my experienced hands over her body A woman can't impregnate another woman I crossed the promontories of her hips and breasts I entered into her veins her arteries into her muscles guts her hips her lungs her heart her liver her spleen and into her spine of iron and dead children's bones We were one body made of two bodies fused in the love that pervaded us that night one late spring in a bloody April above the skies of the Lombard lowlands Already I saw in my mind's eye the fourth great feast in the history of the restaurant Da Rosa Already I was preparing myself to put my hands to work and make the casseroles with broccoli cheese prosciutto ricotta peas and sausage and carrots and potatoes and spinach and timbales of pastry filled with tagliolini dressed in sage butter wine béchamel and thyme and sage and rosemary mixed with thin strips of chicken and Gallura cockerels and Olivier salads and soufflés and frittatas with onion broccoli spinach potatoes rapini escarole basil zucchini eggplant and rose petals and omelets with prosciutto parmesan and ricotta and vegetables and crepes with sweet cream and chocolate and nuts dusted with cocoa and powdered sugar and preserves: peach apricot currant lemon rose orange The citrus trees that overlook this sea finite flayed furrowed by ships carrying centuries gold millennia wines spices oils handicrafts freemen slaves This sea struck by waves by lights which never forgets a vessel a lighthouse a house This sea of buried dead And back come the millennia and centuries past the buried and reanimated dead and dark women hunched shrunken They weave cloth by the sea They wait rip stitch add rip hook gather They give substance to the sea A sea written drawn corporeal They make it the open closed body of the age-old sea barred with columns with vessels with lighthouses Sea of war sea of earth paper sea of flesh paper Egyptian Sicilian African sea Italian sea Sea of Spain France Greece Albania Roman sea inked handcrafted articulated sea fatigued never tired of setting forth Mediterranean

I saw myself making more hens in broth and roasted geese and beef stew and roasted ox lamb pork veal set over the fire to brown and pastiera and millefoglie and teste di moro and sfogliatelle and mostaccioli and cassata and struffoli and Christmas ciambelle and Easter ciambelle and chocolate salami which you make by mixing crumbled cookie and cocoa powder and ground coffee and rum and sugar and ground walnuts almonds hazelnuts rolled up into a fat snake and dusted with cocoa and powdered sugar And cannoli filled with ricotta blended with melted sugar candied fruit chopped nuts and bittersweet chocolate flakes and homemade cannoli pasta filled with ground meat and prosciutto and cheese and ricotta and béchamel and Neapolitan sfogliatelle made by folding a very thin layer of pastry dough a thousand times until you have a shell or a pubis filled with ricotta candied fruit melted sugar and chocolate flakes and Santa Rosas filled with yellow cream and whipped cream with a core of black cherry jam which is the sweetest and most sensual pastry there is and chocolates made by pouring into molds dark chocolate around a core of rice or pistachio or almond paste and pastry cream and coffee cream thick enough not to spill out and soft chocolates made by mixing crumbled cookies and cocoa powder and rum and then sprinkling them with coffee powder and powdered sugar

After our first afternoon of love at the Certosa in Vigevano I ordered to the room bird-shaped chocolates that filled the hollow of a sweet mound of sugar sponge cake ricotta rum and sugar

To me she seemed like a fair little mermaid like the mermaid on the port in Copenhagen condemned to be a siren by day and a woman by night so great was the division between dark and light that no mortal could love her She floated on the sea's deep surface I caressed her breasts I caressed her body which had become one with mine She lay limply under the shroud of sheets damp with bodily humors and sweat The chocolate from the little birds dribbled from the corners of her little mermaid mouth I put her hands in mine—Reader—It was the miracle of the host repeated in the form of love It was the transubstantiation of bodies the metamorphosis of food in flesh and the transubstantiation of one flesh into another Of one flesh into another like what happened to the Nazarene when he drank the bitter chalice of blood and glorious poulticed human flesh A God come to earth a miracol mostrare the way my little mermaid manifested with her opulent beauty in whose forms the miracle of God was legible We abandoned ourselves to the indulgence of pleasure of oblivion of forgetting With our sexes in our interlocked hands we closed our eyes until the next morning I covered her naked body with the sheets stained with wine liqueur and chocolate Her dark little crown rested like the peak of a dark black mountain of desire on the embroidered pillowcase like the ones I'd inherited from my mother We slept in the warmth of the balminess of the room where the condensation from our breaths vaporized on the windows luminescent with artificial light and frost

We slept until late morning the next day We went down for breakfast in the blue-brocaded dining room into which filtered the pale late spring sunlight of a bloody April in lowland Lombardy We ordered croissants filled with cream and steaming-hot milk with coffee and cocoa powder over the thick white froth and toast with butter and preserves of orange and lemon and strawberry and plum and blueberry and fig and black cherry and rose and basil and all the citrus that grows along the eternal shores of this sea finite flayed furrowed by ships carrying centuries gold millennia wines spices oils handicrafts freemen slaves This sea struck by waves by lights which never forgets a vessel a lighthouse a house

I watched her as the milk froth hit her like a wave of seafoam and I saw the blood-colored preserves dribble from her little rosebud mouth She sank her pearly white Chinese teeth into slices of bread with sugar and cinnamon and butter and preserves that she dipped in the thick milk cream It was a pleasure to see this communion of matter this transubstantiation of flesh and food

I watched the pale sky outside turn even paler in the sun of the Po Lowlands We were sitting at the breakfast table and the smell of caffè latte and tea and cream and toast and cookies emanated from the plates and the teapots and the pewter and silver and fine porcelain creamers Other guests were sitting at the tables Among them was a woman alone as

dark as a Greek kore Alone like the lone woman in the Hopper
painting I liked her I love all women—Reader—I sleep alone
When I die I'll bring my living and my dead all the struffoli
tarts beignets savory pies fried pizzelle that I learned from
my mother's age-old art I'll lay at the feet of the angels and
God my roasts my stews broccoli pasta wine-braised sausages cassata roccocò mostaccioli pasta with ragù pasta with
pesto sautéed vegetables stuffed chickens and turkeys hen
in broth with celery carrot and potato stuffed suckling pig
thrush with polenta rapini with garlic Olivier salad vitel tonnè
shrimp cocktail green salad mayonnaise vegetables agrodolce
stuffed peppers eggplant mushroom-style with tomatoes and
garlic and eggplant-zucchini parmesan with mozzarella tomato
and parmesan and roasted peppers in oil garlic and parsley
meat-stuffed zucchini broth with butter fried chicken roasted
chicken goose au gratin pork cutlets with rosemary-roasted
potatoes and boiled potatoes and cannoli made with dough
wrapped around metal tubes fried and filled with silky ricotta
mixed with melted sugar candied fruit chocolate chips and
wheat berries pastiera made with ricotta and orange blossom
and sponge cake layered with pastry cream and chocolate
cream I will lay at the feet of God and the feet of my living
and my dead T-bone steaks and chicken cutlets and veal cutlets and sautéed beef liver with golden onions and grilled
pork liver cooked in caul fat with rosemary thyme and sage
browned in oil butter and onion and green bean potato salad
and San Marzano tomato salad with anchovies salt oil parsley
oregano olives and cubes of buffalo mozzarella and fresh mozzarella and margherita pizza and Camogliese pizza and puffed
rice folded into chocolate honey rum and candied fruit and
hazelnuts and almonds to make chewy torrone and rice pilaf
and soufflé of onions potatoes tomatoes peppers and roasted

eggplant and spaghetti with clams and carbonara with egg prosciutto and pancetta and bread with butter and sugar and bread with garlic oil and tomato and cocoa-dusted ricotta and Valtellina pizzoccheri blanched with potatoes spinach chard and dressed with butter oil parmesan sage thyme and bay leaf and cheese pies and crepes with marmalade and frittatas with vegetables with cheese and basil and pies with artichokes peas cabbage and potatoes baked in shortcrust and glorious Caprese cakes with almonds and rum and chocolate I will sit at the feet of the celestial thrones and offer the angels and demons and God Santa Rosa sfogliatelle and cannoli fried sheep brain and veal and artichokes and cabbage and golden-fried zucchini and trays of steamed artichokes with garlic and parsley and oil in their tender hearts and golden-fried artichokes and golden-fried zucchini and eggplant and roasted eggplant stuffed with pasta and meat and roasted eggplant stuffed with old bread mixed with water capers tomatoes cubes of mozzarella and parmesan until the breadcrumb surface turns golden and pieces of buffalo mozzarella in their glorious milk and rapini and rabe and rice balls with meat and ragù and peas and potato croquettes and shortbread cookies and beignets stuffed with meat and with pastry cream and the glory that is the Neapolitan pastiera with orange blossom-infused ricotta and cassata with pistachio and almond paste glaze candied fruit and ricotta and thousands upon thousands of trays filled with cakes made with layers of cream and glaze and chocolate and thousandfold millefoglie made by alternating layers of thin sheet pastry with layers of cream with butter and cream and powdered sugar and chocolate torrone made by pouring into molds chocolate almonds hazelnuts and whipped egg and pumpkin pasta and tagliolini in broth and in sauce and pappardelle and ravioli with walnut sauce and trofie with Ligurian pesto creamed with

milk and meat ravioli and pumpkin ravioli and ravioli with
cheese and ricotta and meat tagliolini in broth and spinach-
ricotta ravioli in sage and butter and potato prosciutto mozzarella and cheese gateaux and thousands upon thousands of
breaded mozzarellas and sautéed rabe and escarole pies made
by stuffing trays of dough made with lightly sautéed escarole
with pine nuts and raisins and a dash of salt and baked on low
until golden brown and beef stew made by putting in cold water
celery onion potato with shank bone and fat shoulder meat a
piece of stew beef and all the spices thyme sage oregano parsley
capers basil which are the glory of the Mediterranean garden
and little plates of Brussels sprouts and cabbage dressed with
ribbons of anchovy and sardines and parsley oil basil and green
and black Gaeta olives and fried marinated anchovies and fried
mozzarella and fresh mozzarella garnished with San Marzano
tomatoes with garlic basil and oil and bread with butter and
jam and bread with butter and sugar and bread with butter and
tuna and cups of milk and cookies and malt and hard friselle
softened in water and topped with diced fresh tomato and basil
and oil and salt and mozzarella and fiordilatte and sugary fried
doughnuts and buttery pastries and purees of meat and flour
and vegetables or broth and fish I made for my daughter when
she was a baby and little pastries made in the shape of little
breasts or horns or golden hills and almond cookies and pasta
casseroles and turkeys with sausage-chestnut stuffing and
other meats and ricotta and peas This will be my glory that I lay
at the feet of God and the feet of my living and my dead I will
fill with the pleasures of the belly the cosmos-sheet on which
life is frescoed I will lay at God's feet my lone and infinite
domesticitude in my cooking diffused under the skies of the Po
Lowlands This has been my talent My God Love me God Love
me for all eternity I have scattered the flavors and scents of

my cooking across the world Accept my gift—Reader—I have fought my battle in life with food I've erected to the heavens cathedrals of pastry and baked longing and pleasure Accept my gift—Reader—I am only a woman I sleep alone

She looked at me as if searching for a solution to her life I looked at both women I felt divided between that austere and swarthy and saturnine beauty and my soft pretty little lady Already I saw myself making love to the dark woman I broke through my hesitation and asked her right out where she was from She lived in Monticelli but had a solitary life I'd never seen her before I told her I would come visit her one day and I invited her to Da Rosa My little lady looked at me jealously I didn't want to disturb the peace of our little transubstantiated love We went out to have another coffee and a cigarette That day I would take her to Chiaravalle Abbey whose tall Gothic church tower stood out in the skies of the Po Lowlands among springs docks dams canals and rows of poplars oaks maples birches The church stood in the decrepit spring morning on a bloody April that raged in the lunar landscape of a plain once devastated by Huns Visigoths and Longobards who pillaged the riches of the empire concentrated in its churches abbeys and castles where the feudal lords gathered monks and travelers and pilgrims and foreign warriors to battle enemies and bishops thundered from pulpits against sacrilege ignominy heresy and managed the affairs of the towns and villages We went to one of those glorious abbeys founded in Chiaravalle in the High Middle Ages which stood with its imposing walls with mullioned windows and slender lesenes lined with a divine lunar light that became human in the human light We entered through a wide door into a space with three naves separated by a wide colonnade supporting rib vaults and pointed spires We explored the interior leaving traces of our hands on the colonnades And hands were all over the columns and the hippogriffs and fish and swans and mermaids and demons and angels and fish and birds on the Gothic and Corinthian capitals Our one body disintegrated and left traces the way Huns and Visigoths and Lombards who had razed then repopulated the plains around Mediolanum making a contrada of the empire into Longobardia a region bustling with trade and commerce with the South of the world with Florence with Rome with Tunis with Libya and with the kingdoms of the Franks and the Teutons and the Flemish merchants

It was cold We took refuge in a remote restaurant in the middle of an old farm estate surrounded by expanses of endless green grass in the pale moonlike sun and granaries farmyards and canals and poplars maples birches We ordered steaming-hot chicken soup with crostini and melted fontina We ordered fondue We dipped meat and bread into the boiling red green yellow amaranth sauces of fontina gorgonzola liqueur tomato ragù melted green cheese The boiling sauces that warmed the veins running though our bodies and organs like hot rivers of dense vapor of hot blood running in droplets at the corners of my beautiful lady's mouth I could feel our flesh merging into one I took her plump little hand She was a spoiled child but open to surprises and life's pleasures when she was delivered of the stifling boredom of her house where she was made prisoner to a room prey to the restless dust of time Perhaps she loathed and feared the noise and the farmyard traffic the way I feared the thunderous roar of the vacuum reminding us that time has its infernal rhythm of works and days we're all trying to escape To give ourselves over to life soft and slow we ate a rich puree of potatoes with ricotta butter egg and béchamel and fried polenta in different shapes accompanied by little Lombard sausages and strips of pork loin au jus

I recalled our hands in the abbey on the moonlike plain and I savored the succulent foods and the rough Florentine linen napkins and Flanders linen tablecloth Around us in the plain farmhouse restaurant immersed in the thick mist of heat of the smells of milk coffee wine desserts and liqueurs with just a few fellow diners We all ate silently intently as if the high thick spartan walls and towering ceilings prompted entering into a mystical and entranced pleasure My silent lady looked at me childlike A gleam of joy shone deep in her eyes The trip was giving us back our joy And perhaps now that my mind was occupied with a new woman she was falling in love with me It had been so long since I'd fallen in love and her sweet gaze on my hands and my face took me back to my mother's hands taking care of little me and tucking me in cozy and tender and telling me an old fairy tale Again I felt the hands of Marina and of Tina navigating my body as if sailing across a storm-tossed sea We stared at each other solemn and slow in the vapors that billowed out from the kitchen where we saw the roasts sizzling They sizzled sending the scents of meat and fried potatoes and roasted potatoes and potato skins all aromatic cooking on the grill There was a huge fireplace in stone and marble with a pair of bas-reliefs a Visconti and a Sforzesco

After the meat my lady sank her teeth into a testa di moro which is soft sponge cake with a gooey chocolate-and-rum filling covered in cocoa powder and sprinkles It was a creamy confection enamored with itself for bringing joy to those who ate it She stood up and ran her hand along the stone and marble mantel over which glimmered a seventeenth-century pendulum clock with gold cherubs on each side with curlicues and curves in mother-of-pearl enclosing a clock-heart stopped forever at the same time conserving the secrets of the past It stopped centuries ago at the sight of a noblewoman with her lover murdered by her jealous husband who stabbed a dagger into her heart The ancient blood stained the clock which remained a silent witness of lost time having been witness to a time that no longer exists It was a precious object that shone in the austere and dark surroundings of the vast room bathed in the pale sunlight falling over the Lombard plains We ordered wine grappa coffee liqueur and rosolio We were warm with satisfaction and affection Now and then I thought of the dark serious severe woman alone like the lone woman in the Hopper painting looking at me across the distance of the memory of the night before As I treacherously squeezed my pretty little lady's hand I imagined her trim and tall form dark and severe I saw her as a sequence of sharp and severe forms of promontories of gulfs and dark mounds on which shone the reflection of the light tracing half-moons on her Latin woman's skin She was a woman of the South maybe of Sicilian or Norman or Tunisian origin I learned that she was from Lecce

I resumed looking with eyes that couldn't lie at my little Lombard China girl who read the signs of betrayal on my face But we didn't want to think about the future and I didn't want to lock her life and mine and the sky and the stars and God away in a tower We reemerged to see the stars and sun and moon of the day that began to wane covering over with fog and the unconfessed crimes that were committed every day in secret in the houses of the rich industrialists and merchants of Padania

For an instant I felt she was in danger too but I knew her husband would never deprive himself of the ornament of such a gracious gentlewoman She started to depend on me In truth I could love the woman from the South without rejecting the woman from the North In the China girl's features I saw the contours of the promontories and gulfs of Campania with its

Oriental and Spanish touch imprinted on her little ears her hair with its smooth and shiny part The gulfs the promontories the southern woman's curves brought me back to Mitigliano to Ieranto to Sant'Agata to Positano to Li Galli to my youth when Marina and I would go to Torca and Turchillo like little devils running through the meadows like little demons running through the fields of tomatoes artichokes radishes lettuces cabbages beets zucchini and fig trees lemon trees orange trees and grapevines In wafted the warm scent of the timbale of potatoes onions peppers oil and tomato and garlic and basil that we made to save money That frugality passed down by our parents remained in my blood I'm parsimonious with my clothes too what few I have but I don't skimp on food or tableware or the beauty of my trattoria

The southern woman embodied the languid musk of the sun-drenched afternoons on the Gulf of Naples when the traffic and noise of the Spanish Quarter resume after the midday break The little shops reopen with their grains their shimmering fish their mandarins oranges tomatoes pineapples cantaloupes canary melons yellow and green and orange peppers zucchini eggplants white red and black cabbage chard turnip greens broccoli rabe carrots onions shallots arugula escarole lettuce peaches cherries apricots strawberries currants blueberries Bosc and Williams and Abate pears table grapes green grapes red grapes Isabella grapes Capri grapes Lombard grapes and blackberries and walnuts and tapioca and almonds and hazelnuts and peanuts and mangoes and fresh chestnuts and roasted chestnuts and fresh figs and chocolate-covered figs and figs filled with nuts And fabric shops with their textiles wool silk brocade linen cotton canvas nylon jute in all the colors of the rainbow And in the bars and cafés resumes the life that in the sun-drenched midday break had seemed dead in the strident voice of the chaos of the pulverized life of the world silent with longing behind the shutters where men and women take respite from the quotidian and the harm that life causes is stopped on the face of the boundless clock of time Time no longer exists

Nor did it exist that afternoon when the twilight shadows fell slowly on the quiet plain We could hear water rushing through the little canals along the road from the farmhouse to the car All was still in the incipient magic evening but it was only five in the afternoon Cruising through the landscapes of frost and mist with the twinkling first stars led by Hesperus lady of the threshold between day and night We reached Vigevano We went down to the Pensione Certosa I took her upstairs the way you do with a little girl who as an effect of love seemed more self-aware and less spoiled Slow we opened the door to the room where the panels of the walls cast their own absence I undressed her slow and soft kissing her little lips and mouth that still exuded warmth love and food We were repeating the miracle of the host It was the transubstantiation of one material into another of one body into another body of one creature into another of one nature into another We were flesh of one flesh My mind left the gun and drifted to the constellations of the South and the North that always came together in the compass rose under my mother's sacred feet I was already thinking of work I would make fondue and roast and pasta in red sauce I needed to go shopping for groceries We lay back and tired we fell asleep until evening when we had a dinner of ricotta tortelli in steaming-hot broth and desserts and coffee and liqueurs I paid the bill That night we made the long trip back I left her in the silent farmyard where tools and tractors stood silent casting long shadows into the night sleeping under a sky of stars obscured by light fog and frost-dust I sent her off saying I'd be back The next morning I went shopping at the supply warehouses next to the husband's farm full of traffic and trade and men and women and children playing in the sun carrying their chocolate eggs It was a massive art deco building with big windows ornamented in Jugendstil bas-relief friezes Inside there were huge counters with glittering fresh fish: scorpionfish mullets cockles wedge clams and smooth clams and swordfish and tuna made a spectacle alongside the vegetables

I bought the thrushes I needed to go with the polenta I looked around The vast black floor was all wet It was so cold under the high wide vaults of the immense ceiling with cranes and hooks dangling quarters of ox of lamb of sheep of goat and veal rabbit chicken waiting to be skinned and frozen A great cacophony of voices spread from north to south of the immense space as I thought of the North and South painted on the faces of my two loves for whom that evening I was going to prepare polenta with the thrushes roasted over the fire drizzled with oil and rum served with potatoes and a loaf of polenta and a roast en croute made by roasting tender veal round in a casserole with oil butter milk rosemary and thyme and then covering it with dough brushed with egg to make it golden brown I looked all around walking from one stand to the next I bought the yellow flour for the polenta I was going to make by mixing the cornmeal with ricotta water broth butter a dash of salt and béchamel to make it silky and creamy and velvety I bought shelled and unshelled walnuts hazelnuts almonds and salad: endive arugula shallot lettuce and potatoes for the sides I bought white flour for the tortelli and eggs for the tagliatelle I was going to use in an eggplant pasta dish with alternating layers of eggplant ricotta mozzarella and fried eggplant and layers of tagliolini in fresh tomato sauce and basil and oil and béchamel I bought cocoa for the Caprese cake I was going to make once again mixing toasted ground almonds with cocoa rum potatoes ricotta coffee beaten egg whites and egg yolks blended with sugar and milk and then baked for thirty minutes and ricotta and potato flakes to make it dense and moist not crumbly or loose like the delicate sponge cake I would make I was also going to make a coffee-based dessert alternating layers of mascarpone mixed with egg whites and infused with coffee and rum and layers of coffee-dipped ladyfingers and coffee-rum-soaked sponge cake with big flakes of chocolate stuffed with layers of whipped cream

I spent nearly all the money I'd brought impressed by the market's sumptuous abundance I had decided to honor the two of them at Da Rosa that night Then I would take them both on a trip to Vigevano to the Pensione Certosa

Evening was still a ways off I took a break from kitchen work to visit the southern woman who lived alone I knocked at the door and she showed me to a sparsely furnished grand foyer It was a little two-story house like mine not far from town It was perched on a low Longobard hill where there used to be a small Longobard throne in a Norman church that had been deposited there when the Longobards fought in the First Crusade when Italy was still divided into Municipalities which would become little City-States grown out of the cross-breeding of barbarians and bourgeoisie and the Latin vulgus

Only a few stones remained of that ancient structure containing the marble throne adorned with bas-reliefs that stood beside its door Inside the house was spacious dark harsh austere like its mistress Only a few pieces of furniture ornamented the bare walls of bare stone It was an old house without plaster without color It was a house made of stone like its mistress who was made of black lava of ash dust and lapilli from a volcano that gave life to a woman's black body like the black Madonnas of the South patron saints of birthing mothers and guardians of past present and future generations

She greeted me in a simple black wool dress She wore a red ribbon around her neck which was as pale white as was her face It looked like a streak of blood across her throat Her pallor stood out even more under the olive hue of her silky skin smooth like a pearl under the texture of which her tiny veins and tangle of arteries appeared She led me through the house into the dining room There was a hearth with a fire a simple rustic table of dark walnut with a few chairs and a cabinet with plates and glasses "I too" she said "look after the bones of creation Every morning when I wash the dishes and cups from my solitary breakfast I put away the washed and dried bones of dead children and of stars and constellations and God I too put away the bones of my husband who abandoned me and my children who are grown and far away on their own paths" She gave me the gift of pieces of her story and showed me a house in which order and rigor austerity parsimony reigned unlike the profligate indulgence of my Lombard China girl's Oblomovian lust This new woman who was fifty but whose face suggested less was a vestal virgin of a southern temple She had suffered abandonment and carried its signs on her thin body which bore the traces of the hands of a child and a man who had once sought it "I sleep alone" she said

I looked at her face It was severe but not sad She led me through the bathroom into the bedroom furnished with only a dark mahogany bed with a fire-red cover an old walnut armoire and a red velvet armchair There were no curtains on the windows or paintings on the walls It looked like the house of a cloistered nun If it weren't for the fires in the main rooms we would've shivered with cold like in the halls of an ancestral castle or a cloistered nun's cell She had withdrawn from the public world and from friends and old acquaintances to take refuge in Monticelli where she had found peace from her craving for love and affection for which she was insatiably hungry Now she was calmer She filled her days with reading letters walks She didn't make many phone calls She was living on interest from money she had put into savings after her separation from her children and husband she had long lived apart from Now one lived in Florence one in Paris They almost never saw each other But she in her lone solitude had grown accustomed to the absence of the male world around her

From up close the self-satisfied wealth of those who seem fulfilled by their lives lost its luster She had suffered She was wounded I could see the chasm of an entire life around her Her austere and grave world was eons away from the young Chinese geisha's saccharine scene It takes traversing the skin of another to access their heart and reality

Everything depends on reality—Reader—

I could sense that she too swam in the waters of wordless women I took her hand and told her simply to come to Da Rosa that night I would have Tina or my daughter pick her up She squeezed my hand gently She felt the contact of a woman's hand warming the male universe where she had been chained for a lifetime without love without hope full of terrors anxieties and fears Now the prospect of a lesbian love smiled at her as a way out of her solitude as a woman alone like the woman drinking alone in the Hopper painting She told me she would come on her own She wasn't afraid of walking down State Road 43 alone in the open countryside I left her with no words but a kiss on her thin lips I left that late spring morning in a bloody April and went back to prepare the restaurant for the evening I was expecting my little geisha too I knew she would come with her husband I had made two separate plates of polenta and thrush for my women

Slow and soft fell the evening shadows on the Lombard plain My daughter and Tina helped set the tables with the Flanders linen tablecloths my mother had given me Tina had turned on the infernal vacuum in the kitchen and the hall That rumble out of a circle of hell unleashed the madness of time and of clocks whose faces measure out the span of death and of life Realizing that I loved women my daughter looked at me circumspect She was in the phase of life where you love a man you want to have children and a family The peaceful harbor of lesbian love was alien to her I knew she couldn't understand me I loved her for what she was Taking her hands in mine I said to her "Love me for what I am" I saw in her eyes the light of eternal and divine filiation She loved me anyway since we had made our pact by which I passed down the age-old knowledge of food and hands that I inherited from my mother It was a pact of souls and blood and skin and flesh that no earthly contingency could ever break Heartened by my daughter's clear and godlike gaze I knew I didn't want to lock the sky God and stars away in a tower and now more serene I awaited that evening's guests

At eight that evening slow tawny shadows began to rise in the plain The grave Lombard commensals advanced toward us There would be no more orgies only sacred repasts after pleasure languor and lust By then the men and women had realized the sacred value of food They knew that every day the miracle of the host was repeated by which the material of water earth trees flowers fruit stone dirt animals food becomes the material of the material of flesh and of human bodies

In the sacred atmosphere the commensals entered slow and silent They sat down serious and serene at the tables They had learned to respect themselves the other and food I brought out the meat and the pasta timbales and the polenta with thrushes and the trays of tagliolini with roasted eggplant We served in silence Only the murmur of a few voices and the clinking of silver and crystal could be heard in the general silence The men and women let themselves be filled with a pleasure without excess or overflow letting the heat and the colors of the foods and the wines come over them The God of food who reigned in the dining hall that night was good

With a solemn air like a priestess my woman from the South entered alone followed by my little Chinese geisha and her Romagnan husband The little geisha was escorted by a man who flaunted her like a jewel in his lapel She sat down with him at a secluded table I saw her round hips hugged by a snug silk dress that highlighted her body's curves and made her look like a little siren girl Her red red lips were smothered with violet-red lipstick and lined with brown pencil Her beady jet-black eyes were surrounded by a line of kohl her cheeks dusted with fiery violet rouge It was a harsh and heavy look that made her into a little opulent Botero woman but I liked her for what she was with her vulgar makeup and rich self-satisfied provincial manner of dress I knew how much boredom and bitterness lay behind that makeup that gold jewelry adorning her neck and arms and hands and behind the silks the expensive shoes the earrings that made her into a tacky overdone Christmas tree I felt sorry for that little doll treated with the regard typically reserved for a collector's item not for a creature of God I knew she had found peaceful harbor in our lesbian love so sweet it was to entrust oneself to the arms of an equal without domination without plans without violence without the thought of reproducing building a family or wealth or business So soft and slow purely being together even just to see another's body in your arms and caress it with no penetration but the gentle touch of fingers in the secret recesses of a loveable body with its folds its scars its wrinkles its fat its bones its wounds its richness its poverty its beauty born of reciprocal love She looked at me with a conspiratorial and grateful look Her husband clueless that his pampered little doll allowed herself any amusements besides clothes bonbons furs didn't even glance at the other patrons he was so busy studying the effect made on a generic public by his pretty little jewel and his expensive pinstripe suit and patent leather shoes and thick glossy mustache But in the sacred atmosphere of the dining room that evening there was no room for cheap talk In each and every one the miracle of the host was performed by which the material of flowers fruits trees fields earth water animals contained in the food became the material of the human bodies hunched from their daily labors They ate in silent enjoyment intent on every bite Each was a gift from God and creation In the austere and weighty air of my dining room I could hear sing the harmony of chaos in which matter materializes things thingify humans humanize And God godifies

I brought out an asparagus and spinach cream soup made by mixing the minced cooked vegetables and béchamel and ricotta and broth and milk and mascarpone and fontina and rum Golden croutons floated over the vegetables My beauty's deep red lips pearled with green She was a colorful guileless girl made of erotic languor and abandon to creation I nursed the thought of new love the way you attend to a baby that needs to be cradled cleaned cared for My daughter looked at me She too wanted to enter into the play of conspiratorial gazes between women I wanted to guide her to a peaceful harbor In my head I said to her "Love me my daughter I held you at my breast I nursed you nurtured you cradled you clothed you guided you watched you looked after you raised you blessed you adored you Love me for what I am don't ask me for more Love me the way I love you in the landscape of your France your man your Antibes your bicycle ride to Pavia" I looked at her long and intense with the soup tureens in my hands I saw everything in slow motion and resumed ladling the soup into the shallow bowls My daughter wore a simple black dress My daughter only for a time had enjoyed the realm of fathers Her father died when she was little I raised her alone and school was the only constant in my life In those years all I cooked was minestrone and beef cutlets and grilled or fried fish Who would have imagined then that I would exhume from the drawers of the past my mother's ancient knowledge of food She put a splash of rum in everything the way I do now My delicate rum-laced soups dotted my patrons' lips with green The sacrality dissolved It became an evening of relaxed enjoyment and rest The butcher shop owner chatted with his wife surrounded by his children in-laws and grandchildren I could see the domestic and convivial element of that corner of the secluded and ordinary province where I had taken refuge after the splendor of the landscapes of the South I lost myself in the eyes of the women I loved I collected myself and went into the kitchen to get the trays of tagliolini and eggplant and polenta with thrushes and sausage and wine

Just before nine I saw my southern woman come in shivering in a black coat That lone woman sparked curiosity Little was known about her but that she had arrived a few years ago and at first young men would visit her Now nobody did She was seen shopping for groceries without talking to anyone When she appeared a void formed around her My daughter noticed us exchanging looks She became sullen and jealous The woman in the subtle and austere beauty of her years slid off her coat revealing a simple gray wool dress which she had adorned with

a silver and amethyst brooch She took the soups that I served
I wooed her discreetly offering her bread and wine I was careful that no one would talk in that provincial setting I told her
I would take her to Vigevano In a dangerous move I squeezed
her hand attracting curious looks but I didn't withdraw it and
she felt welcomed like a lady It was an alliance between women
that could have caused talk and conflict but that night I didn't
pay much heed to that My daughter looked jealous I went to
my little lady's table and offered husband and wife the polenta
with thrush The fire crackled in the hearth I looked up at the
windows through which blazed a tremulous fire red It was a
bloody April in the Po Lowlands that now stood silent like
a cradle around my house I didn't want to lock life sky stars
and God in a tower When my China girl got up I murmured
to her by the window There were curious looks All evening
I went back and forth The last logs in the hearth crumbled into
ash spreading the scent of the apple and orange peel sage and
rosemary I'd added to the fire

For dessert I brought out a chocolate mousse made by
blending cocoa coffee grounds rum mascarpone ricotta cream
and egg yolk and sugar and butter and ricotta and whipped egg
whites left to cool in the fridge As my patrons slowly dispersed
my daughter and Tina and I returned to the kitchen to clean
and immediately Tina fired up the vacuum with its frenzied
roar My jealous daughter went into her room I followed her and
said "Daughter love me for what I am Let's give each other the
peace and the sacred alliance between women and living creatures You alone are mine" I cradled her in my arms and put her
to sleep like I did when she was little telling her the fairy tale
about the jade-green bird She closed her eyes serene with her
hands in mine I went back down to the kitchen and scrubbed
the pans washed the dishes tidied up put the leftovers in

the fridge It was one in the morning I went upstairs to sleep and I sent Tina off with a big hug The night stood silent with demons elves and angels of God

The next morning I decided to take a walk alone through the fields illuminated by a late afternoon blood spring sun in Southern Lombardy Silently I said to my daughter "You're my queen I want to keep you with me in my house" The fields were slow in the dust of time that settles on all the things of the time in which you live in chaos in which things thingify nature naturalizes creatures creaturize humans humanize And God godifies After my walk alone through the fields where I took delight in immersing myself in the poppies and the rice taking off my shoes because it was already late spring and looking into the pale absolute light of the sun that lives inside things that exist even without being seen I headed home In the kitchen I prepared breakfast for us three lone women My daughter Tina and I sat at the table to eat a plain crostata and a marmalade crostata apricot peach mandarin orange blueberry strawberry currant chestnut banana orange lemon plum and bread and butter and jam and powdered sugar toasts and warm milk We savored that food with the favor of the gods who looked down on us from above in a sign of utmost respect for the lives that are forged in the benevolent milk of the gods that live in the chaos that surrounds all things I watched the slow houses outside dissolving into slow volutes of dust and smoke The bread was soft in our mouths that savored the food amid slow smoky thoughts When breakfast was finished I said to my daughter "You are a queen You are the queen of my house I am for you alone I will carry you with me into my house"

I walked over to my southern love's house where she awaited me naked and silent in the low building in striped white and black stone that stood out against the naked stone overflowing into the ramparts of the sky I cried with joy and pain for what I had and I thanked God who told me go on warrior keep going walk Give in to your life and your death that will never leave you in your life

The southern woman whose name was Edda told me "Just a minute" I saw her dress slow in her room The bedroom was designed like a Gothic cathedral extending toward the sky its spires its points its rosettes its tall thin lesenes I saw her naked with her promontories in profile like peaceful harbors in her life and mine I didn't want to lock her life or my life or the sky stars and God away in a tower Naked she was beautiful and tragic in the absolute nudity that lives inside the things that exist without being seen Her inviolate body said to me Love me I am only for you I went to the bed and I bent and bent to lick her pubis and her siren girl's lips as she moaned in my arms over loves past present and future She wanted to be only for me We loved each other for what we were We were free We said sweet and tender words to each other as we ate tarts with chocolate and black cherry and apricot and blueberry and currant and chestnut and fig and peach We wiped our flushed lips We watched the splendor of thunder that rose in the sky that appeared and disappeared in the mist of the Po Lowlands The South upon contact with a North bright with frost that said "You're for me alone" Her dress fell slow over the slender hips slow with desire She told me "My love take me with you into your house" She was beautiful and happy in her nakedness full of desire and longing that came together in my outstretched hands in hers We were in love and happy I wiped the jam at the corners of her lips She was happy to exist as a star of creation Chaos sang in the harmony in which things thingify matter materializes creatures creaturize nature naturalizes and God godifies We went to the door where a pale April sun awaited us saying "Be happy enjoy life that smiles at those who know how to look at it with the serene eyes of a child" I knew that my domesticitude was a gift from God No one could take it from me not loves not landscape not even God not stars not dust nor Bellatrix Arcturus Alhena nor Castor Pollux Antares nor Crater Corvus Canis nor Auriga Andromeda Pisces not even the deepest pits not deep wild waters whether wells whether rivers whether seas not human plant animal whether born grown dead not deserts not walls whether high whether low whether long whether narrow neither past nor future not rotations not revolutions not celestial bodies nor solar systems not even galaxies nor earth nor sky not even beings works and days not sea not coasts neither winds nor breezes not destinations not ships not docks not even lightning nor star storms not Austro not Borea not water not earth not land whether promised whether burnt whether destroyed not even no man's nor foreign nor chosen nor home not even going returning leaving settling digging nor mountains nor plains heaths hills whether cultivated arable uncultivated neither fat nor skinny nor gray nor black nor red neither rich nor poor and dry neither stars whether variable whether new whether pulsating double dwarf giant not even falling spinning twinkling crinite nor comets whether blue yellow orange neither wandering nor Milky Ways not peace not war not dust not even Arcturus Vega Capella not deuterons protons electrons not even interplanetary pull not even phonons not dust not even voices neither dead nor born nor hadrons bosons fermions not even charmonium gluons neutrons nor partons protons much less rishons not even colors not even enchantment not even blood not even orbits not motion not truths not even ghosts not even enchanted not even strange

After eating and getting dressed between the bare walls of the house where she lived alone like the woman who drinks alone in the Hopper painting we went out in the pale April sun We saw the clouds darken with the storm that illuminated the Lombard landscape in which sail the deciduous queens of heaven saying to me "Go on warrior keep going walk move Give in to the life in your death Then stop Look behind you Don't regret anything Your life has not been in vain You've spent it well You did what you could Don't give up keep going warrior walk on Life is long It's worth it It's worth it Life is worth it Death is worth it You've spent your life well It hasn't been in vain You did what you could Carry it your belly like a port of desire—your life a baby Keep it well Make it a gift from God that protects you from up in the heavens"

Her body was beautiful and happy in the Lombard heaths over which paraded the low-lying deciduous queens of heaven saying "This is a child as glorious as the primordial fetus" We said to each other "Love me I'm yours for eternity" I looked at her and she looked at me lovingly but I knew my daughter was jealous A conflict of wants and complex plots that offered its tangle of suspicions up to heaven I didn't mind seeing the sky of my life become darker and cloudier I didn't want to lock up my life under a low thin ceiling I wanted to go my own way which told me go on warrior keep going walk Keep your life inside you like a gift from the gods

4

I wanted to follow my own path which told me go on warrior keep going walk Keep your life inside you like a gift from the gods I wanted to deflect all conflict It was early The night still heralded an overcast sky Flashes of thunder dissolved in the light mist that hovered silent in the pleasant morning as the sky cleared Her house stood out in silhouette like a castle of longing in the landscape of the Lombard lowlands where canals rice fields and poplars maples birches extended as far as the eye could see

After dropping off my woman of the South of the world my woman of the soul at her stone house in the misty land-scape of the Po Lowlands all alone in her big house without children without relatives without a companion without even a cat for companionship I went to pick up my little China girl I found her in her kingdom of unquiet dust and tedium and torpid dissatisfaction and lust and greed She was wrapped in a green robe that cast her sinuous silhouette onto the back wall of the dusty bedroom She was eating cookies with jam and toast with butter and offered me some as soon as she saw me She was beautiful like a spoiled little girl kept locked up by her mother out for fear of her ruination The same way her husband preferred to see her segregated rather than lose his precious plaything

Before going out I checked that the stove was off and the windows were closed the way my father used to Like him I was always afraid of theft or fire In his quiet sorrow my father was a lone and anxious man From him I inherited the anxiety of time that was triggered whenever I heard the thunderous rumble of Tina's infernal vacuum which haunted my nights and days and I lived as if always on a razor's edge I told myself "Let it go Rosa don't fall into the spiral of madness forget your gun give yourself over to life" And I saw myself inside a boat sailing the sea with my feet plunged into the depths All I had to do was put aside the cares the troubles the turmoil and dive with a child's wonder-filled eyes into the waves of fate Only a child gives themself over with awe wonder and abandon accepting the pull of the water's gritty sparkle gazing out at the landscape that exists in absolute presence without relying on anything or anyone else The ship of my life sailed the surface of the seas without mastery over death or life From the surface of the still absolute seas I returned to the room over the farmyard Outside traffic trade and commerce buzzed in the pale sun that rose high in the sky The husband haggled with the local industrialists

She started getting ready slipping into a plush dress made of silk and soft dusty periwinkle violet-gray wool She knew we were going to Vigevano but we had to wait for her husband to step out Just before noon he left We went downstairs She scuttled in high heels like a Chinese hen in a henhouse She was funny and sweet and soft a dandelion in a world of wars battles conflicts and storms a world without peace We crossed the yard quickly passing children playing with a ball and with the farm animals while nibbling on chocolate eggs

After Vigevano I was planning to prepare food and the dining room at Da Rosa for a special new evening I didn't know if it would be a sacred repast or a massive feast but I didn't trouble myself about it for the moment I was leaning into my loves Way up high in the high high sky of Padania the sun climbed pulling in its chariot the deciduous queens of heaven who put on an opulent pageant of lesser gods little putti hippogriffs gryphons erinyes unicorns around Helios's chariot that raced high whipping the horses of the sun

We hopped into my little car She crossed her plump legs Everything about her the skin the shoes the dress shone and her soft jasmine perfume infused the air inside the car carefully cleaned with Tina's vacuum We traveled in silence past rows of maple trees poplars oaks birches and dams and docks and canals and rice fields and water fountains and granaries and barns and farms We came to Edda's house where she was waiting in the quiet large stark gloomy dim room She greeted us with a placid expression but a hint of tension in her languid dark eyes My little China girl was anxious too To allay the tension I made something to eat I made a steaming-hot pasta with a béchamel sauce by mixing in a pot flour starch butter ricotta fontina and rum and finally I poured it into a tureen filled with ziti and maltagliati al dente

We sat down to eat in the sacred space of her dim spartan and sparse dining room where the pale lunar sun of a bloody April in a late spring in the Po Lowlands streamed through the windows The meal warmed our bodies and wayward souls After the pasta we had cheese and bread and drank wine and rum punch with powdered-sugar cookies We spoke little We let the food perform the miracle of the host by which things become things and through food two bodies and fleshes are made one body and one flesh Matter materializes nature naturalizes humans humanize And God godifies

Then we set back off in the car with the vision of wordless things We felt more sororal and loving of ourselves in the peaceful harbor of lesbian love We arrived in Vigevano around three in the afternoon at the Pensione Certosa where we were received by a courteous concierge who asked us if we wanted a queen with a bath We did and he led us to room 53 It was a blue and red room like number 52 We entered in silence We were tired No paintings just red flowers on the bedside table We had them bring some warm milk and rum and cookies and toast with jam which we ate our hearts peaceful We lay down in bed naked without touching The heat from our bodies and breath was enough to make us feel love It was divine being side by side in the calm pleasure and oblivion of God I said to myself "Keep going warrior walk on give yourself over to life" And I saw myself and I saw the boat of my life with the name Rosa on the side That was my name I gave it to myself It crossed the surface of the seas to give over into life It was sweet to be together in carnal contact without even our hands grazing Toward eight we went out slow and easy I took them to a restaurant with a big garden The last rays of the setting sun filtered through the wisteria and ivy on the pergola We ordered boiling-hot broth with pumpkin tortelli meat ricotta prosciutto and spinach The broth was dotted with cream We gazed at each other without a word Without speaking we gazed at the green pergola cool with green leaves and creepers and wisteria and baby's breath and ivy and geraniums Few diners were out at that hour The proprietor and cook went back and forth carrying meats and roasts and bread and wine and spaghetti all'amatriciana made with a sauce of fresh tomatoes basil garlic hot pepper and oregano sautéed in oil We ordered some too feeling the little inferno of spice in our throats parched by the pleasure of proximity and the food Already I was picturing coming down to the cool veranda in the morning for breakfast We went for a little walk in the frost of mist and fog and crime of the Po Lowlands in the silent voices of the rice fields the granaries the barns the docks the canals and the farms

We slept in a silent embrace of mute bodies three bodies in one embraced by the arms of God We were wives lovers sisters We closed our eyes no violence no penetration We luxuriated in the peace of the fleeting moment We were abandoned to life and the waves of fate ferrying us silent over the surface of the seas The morning after we went down for breakfast on the veranda which was so different in its cool green silence compared to the dark austere red restaurant space where I had taken my little China girl We wanted nothing but bright landscapes inside and out to cradle our love We had them bring us bread butter jam and warm milk and croissants and pastries bursting with cream Edda broke the silence first asking Caterina about her life She replied "I'm alone, I live on a big farmstead My husband leaves me alone I spend my days behind shutters in a life of dust and disquiet and boredom I loved myself in my house of dust and longing where I'm always alone without even a dog or cat to keep me company I dissolve into my unquiet dust like a pale moonlight Oblomov I just eat bonbons bread and butter and jam and toast with powdered sugar Every so often someone maybe my husband maybe no one maybe the housekeeper brings me beer-brined Gallura cockerel roasted in coarse salt After the salt roasting it's left to marinate in a beer broth I see my shadow cast on the walls I look fat misshapen wide as if I had hit the bottom of the abjection that disfigures me and brutalizes the Lombard landscape" She looked at us her eyes avid with want She was the first to speak When Caterina fell silent Edda said "I live alone I have no help or children to rely on I have no one to take care of me When someone's there to take care of you it's like being a child home sick from school

The whole world starts to spin around you like Aladdin's lamp or a kaleidoscope like in *Fanny and Alexander* or Proust projecting its light and shadow on the walls You curl up under the covers and don't feel the oppressive weight of the outside world with its blaming and punishments You can watch your mother bring you orange juice poached apple warm broth and be at peace with yourself" As she spoke we ate toasts with butter Caterina had filled a plate with butter cheese and ham sandwiches Our initial hunger sated we drank milk and ate cream and chocolate and pistachio croissants on the cool veranda where ivy myrtles wisteria and hawthorn and baby's breath veiled the Lombard sky that the pale moonlike sun had embroidered with frost

The sun was the God of that dark time we spent in a place that became sacred silent and light we didn't speak and let little sips of steaming tea and milk and coffee enter our souls soothed by whipped cream on hot chocolate We knew all that food would turn into fat and food for the future but for two days we set aside all our chains Our warmed cheeks flushed and our hands moved soft and light It was a continuous bringing and taking of plates cups and glasses emptying teapots and filling milk jugs and coffee pots There were profiteroles made by filling little golden puffs with pastry cream spiced with rum and powdered sugar and chopped almonds They floated on a sea of melted chocolate infused with rum coffee and chopped toasted almonds like in my Mediterranean mother's recipe

Distant was the thought of wives mothers children lovers brides husbands relatives friends We loved each other for what we were We were three bodies one single body of three creatures one creature of three materials one material of three natures one nature of three things one single thing

Transubstantiation still happens It was the miracle of the host that is repeated every day every hour of life filled with despair with desire with longing with bridges with roads with constellations galaxies planets cosmos in destruction in formation and quanta and quarks and rishons and protons and particles all of them strange enchanted phantoms

They brought us more food: sfogliatelle and cookies and sweets frosted with powdered sugar dissolved in water with chocolate and pistachio to form a dense opalescent glaze that melted in the love-hungry mouths that softly grazed for first kisses After the chaste love of the first night at the Pensione Certosa in Vigevano we now made our first timid advances We were girls at their first erotic encounter enacted in a slow play of love that touches them down to the soul which then shrinks upon contact with outside things

After an early morning breakfast maybe in spring maybe a bloody April in Southern Lombardy we set off for Morimondo to the old Romanesque abbey out in the middle of the fields granaries barns docks canals and barns and rice fields and maples and poplars and birches and frost then we returned to the Panda cleaned by Tina's infernal vacuum She was jealous when I left She told me she was looking for a man

We set off for Lodi where for the entire afternoon under the porticos of the ovaline piazza we bought shoes and clothes Then we went to Pavia cruising down the long tree-lined road at whose end we could see the stone bridge closed off and packed with merchants and merchandise Under the bridge a few boats were docked among the larches oaks olives alders

It was the lunar landscape of a Lucia taking her boat out to nowhere How lovely and sweet the Lombard landscape is when you're dying We passed by the station and the city center with its old Gothic Baroque Renaissance Umbertine buildings

We came to Belgioioso, the castle with a vast garden that stands as an example of the Renaissance architecture of joy as opposed to the architecture of pain in the subsequent century that so disturbed the souls of men animals and things The architecture of pleasure and joy that we saw before us with its orthogonal and fractal geometries enraptured us in infinite ecstasy The lanes intersected finite infinite crossing under the earth's direction in focal nodes where stone creatures and angels sing and little fountains of pure water spring The joyous space is contained in a massive door of rough metal and stone and finished in a massive door of stone dust and desire The architecture of pleasure and joy was multiplied in the stately palace with its entrance guarded by two stone lions The building's wings extended like a little Versailles where life is lived beneath the weight of the architraves and archivolts of pleasure and joy We walked down those lanes entranced by the miracle of joy and pleasure that made every stone divine We could hear in the chaos a hosanna of glory sung to the Lord God of the armies of the constellations and of dams roads canals offices buildings gas stations of schools hospitals benches animals coffee pots plates eagles oaks tufa carnelian quartz amethyst cobalt kaolin pyrite aluminum iron graphite cement lard butter oil garlic hot pepper

Our feet went light over the gravel paths We exchanged little kisses sparked by the architecture of joy and pleasure

Now and then I thought of the imminent great feast at Da Rosa for which before leaving I prepared baked pasta by mixing a ragù of tomato garlic oil lard butter onion celery and potato infused with wine and rum which I used to coat the lasagne I made with egg pasta I alternated layers of lasagne with layers of prosciutto butter cheese béchamel ricotta and layers of little meatballs béchamel peas and fresh mozzarella I stored it in the fridge

We gave each other little kisses as we walked soft and light awed by the absolute clarity of the sky that saw the maintenance of the bones that grew and grew by the hour like a golem filling up with the joy we saw all around us The deciduous queens of heaven formed a veil over our triangle of love in which we had found a peaceful harbor We took delight in strolling soft and light over the pebbled paths of Belgioioso which overlooked the foggy and soft Pavese landscape which was a simple absolute embodiment of pleasure and joy We headed for the car and saw in the sky the signs of our love that spoke the language of the mad The ship of fools was happening inside us ready to sail the seas challenging the mores of the petty Padania petite bourgeoisie Before going to dinner we decided to keep our love secret We knew how bad the sting of the petty vulgar petite bourgeoisie of Lombardy can be when they find a scapegoat on which to heap their scorn

We went back to Vigevano giving each other little kisses of love on the fingers tired after having left a part of ourselves on the volutes of dust and smoke of the architecture of joy and pleasure we experienced in Pavia We exchanged little kisses on the mouth and cheeks We went up to room 53 It was nine p.m. Maybe it was spring maybe it was a bloody April We undressed each other naked and sincere we stepped under the gush of the steaming-hot water of the bathroom iridescent with vapor rainbows in that sea of aqueous steam we saw the architecture of joy and pleasure that we had experienced in Pavia multiply

We made love under the gushing water of want and blue steam Edda's body with its Latin thinness was like delicate orthogonal architecture Her body was an architectural structure of pain with a Renaissance heart in her hard smooth harsh dark lines which registered the signs of past pain and the immobility of time stopped inside itself in the single and absolute instant of vision like an obstructed Renaissance perspective leading to a focal point you can't escape All the trees roads muscles tendons joints were frozen in an eternal present obstructing the impossible eternity in which human history becomes the history of God Time and space live in the bare single essence of the juncture of the abscissas of time and the ordinates of space Edda's body with its slender Latin beauty was nailed to this cross like an in-between place ready to plunge into the fractal harmony of the cosmos in motion in which the universe chaos man and God seek one another torturously in a process that contains the torment the joy of searching that is life just as life is the love in whose chaotic cradle Caterina's body with its Baroque volutes of curved and sinuous forms joyfully sank Everything in its curvaceous structure was a hosanna to pleasure and the glory of God The architecture of pleasure of pain both reach out to God but in different ways: the first with the icy torment of perfection frozen in time and space the other with the torment of curved and vortical imperfection A form of pain can be read in both but the Renaissance body rejects the orgasm of chaos The Baroque body only enjoys the orgiastic pursuit of chaos in which the heavenly and stellar and earthly spheres sing Edda was colder frozen blocked stern She stood rigid against the tile Inundated with water her caresses were timid Caterina moaned with pleasure and played with the water touching herself and touching us our breasts and our sexes making Edda's body quiver Shyly I admired their orgasms I was the median between the two the observer of our love I mediated between us so that our differing natures didn't fall into conflict We dried off and lay back in bed kissing each other all over hips breasts pubis

I too retained something of my harsh hard dark forms something soft and Baroque in my breasts and my hips and this saved me from the torturous thought that one day I would be alone and dead I saw my house and the restaurant Da Rosa abandoned desolate empty Edda gone Caterina gone my daughter and Tina gone all my work in the kitchen gone Edda soft and slow was warming up in love I abandoned my visions of future solitude and plunged completely into that love triangle Then we dressed and went down to the green covered veranda It was almost eleven We sat down among the wisteria the baby's breath the ivy We ordered tagliolini with salmon in béchamel with rum and shrimp and peas Slow and easy we ate that sacred meal that consecrated our love We felt united before a pagan or Christian altar The grammar of the architecture of pleasure was legible even in the velvety vines They brought us wine grilled mullet and poached salmon with mayonnaise and butter for the mullet with parsley and lemon We exchanged kisses on the lips Far from home we didn't mind indiscreet looks We were a lesbian triad People looked at us curious and scandalized by the kisses With our fingers and forks we shared bites of food And we ate new potatoes in béchamel with shrimp We asked for some hot light consommé Edda's severe Renaissance form wrapped in a soft wool dress became soft

Soft fell the night on the ship of fools that was our love We had moments of sadness in which we were separated abandoned alone in the waves of fate And so we warded off the grim omens The fire in our hearts dwindled in the night air After eating the fish and the potatoes with tuna and béchamel with celery and peas and prosciutto and cheese we asked for a Caprese chocolate cake with ice cream flavored with rum and flakes of dark chocolate Caterina's little mouth glistened with cream We were sated by that slow and sacred repast For an instant of eternal darkness I saw each of us again alone: three separate bodies through food seeking transubstantiation by which the miracle of the host is repeated by which three bodies become one Out of three materials one single material Out of three women one We resumed savoring our sacred food and our love and our Baroque and Renaissance bodies in the fleeting moment that was the sum of as many lives Then we ordered some warm punch A light humid breeze wafted in that reminded me of the sirocco I used to feel in the endless expanses of olive trees where I buried my childhood Even then I knew I slept alone

After dinner we went for a walk and saw in the distance a little Baroque church with its moonlike spirals melded into the gleaming light of the silent moon and the deciduous queens of heaven rising in flight blessing the mother earth mistress of land water rivers fruits minerals animals humans We felt like part of the splendor of the architecture of creation We kissed again It was two in the morning We went in the bedroom and undressed Distant was the thought of home relatives children husbands work We luxuriated in our intermission between the acts of life For a moment a sepulchral air arose from the small cemetery on the roadside with its small stone and marble tombs that were arranged like the floor of a cubic Renaissance interior We immersed ourselves in a Baroque shroud of sheets and blankets We fell asleep The next morning Edda on waking up got even more tangled in the sheets Again in the bonds of love we became from three women one Then we dressed and went down to have breakfast with bread butter jam and toast and shortbread cookies and little toasts with powdered sugar and warm milk and coffee We kissed still unashamed Later we set off on a walk through a nearby town built according to the architecture of pain and the architecture of pleasure underneath which a torment of the pain of living remains legible

Walking along we saw Baroque statues by the thousands spiraling in on themselves like tormented stone shrouds at the feet of God There was a Saint Agatha martyr and a Saint Lucy holding her martyred eyes on a plate and a Saint Agnes with severed breasts It was a calvary shroud of extreme statues twisting like cirrus and storm clouds rotating inward the way Bernini's Saint Theresa is contorted in her ecstasy of light and of stone We followed that calvary of God hand tight in hand we too transubstantiating into marble stone tufa earthly things We were water rock dirt river lake statue woman The kisses we shared made us of three materials into one single material that passed from one to the other through the contact of our breath our throats our flesh traversed by centuries of light We moved light like bodies flowing on those bodies of stone in a single spiral of dust and smoke and vapor The procession of living and dead began its cavalcade through the fields and sky

The sun brightened slow on that bloody April morning in the Po Lowlands The grain and ripe corn bowed at the slightest breeze The landscape was infused with light From the fields we saw a lone little Baroque house that closed on itself like a shell like a bread-dough cathedral containing secret cases of longing built on the architecture of joy and of pleasure found in restless eternal motion We search for God in the time that we die and we live tremendous with joy and with pain and with furor Life is ferment battle struggle joy torment It's never still It is a glorious eternal churning movement in which we were absorbed and celebrated along with our sacred repasts Even breakfast acted as a gentle tremendous vortex of life inside us Hand in hand we came to a town with two rows of facing houses on a long straight road On one side a group of rigid austere bleak harsh dark Renaissance houses in stone marble and bossage precious high sublime in the potency of frozen time The entire street led toward a single tremendous focal point but the right side of that architecture suffered twisting in its orgiastic amorous fervor of Baroque vaults and volutes that devoured space time desire canceling out time in an infinite ecstasy

We traveled all the roads of men and God We entered a Baroque church and left our womanly handprints on the wide columns and naves We reemerged in the pale sun looking at each other full of love We had a box of chocolates with us We exchanged kisses on the mouth greedy with desire We took refuge in a café converted from part of an old farmhouse Through the big window we saw the long parade of the tormented statues of saints and that sublime street with its rows of houses facing off like seven thousand horsemen We asked for hot sandwiches with ham cheese ricotta and red wine We ate slow and easy buttered crostini and sturgeon caviar and salmon roe and fried pastries dusted with cocoa and powdered sugar filled with chocolate and whipped cream and nuts like the ones I would make according to my mother's recipe by mixing egg flour sugar milk butter and yeast into a compact dense and silky dough that we left to rise on the kitchen counter from which we could see the farmer's tractor creeping along the abyss that overlooks this sea finite flayed furrowed by ships carrying centuries gold millennia wines spices oils handicrafts freemen slaves This sea struck by waves by lights which never forgets a vessel a lighthouse a house This sea of buried dead And back come the millennia and centuries past the buried and reanimated dead and dark women hunched shrunken They weave cloth by the sea They wait rip stitch add rip hook gather They give substance to the sea A sea written drawn corporeal They make it the open closed body of the age-old sea barred with columns with vessels with lighthouses Sea of war sea of earth paper sea of flesh paper Egyptian Sicilian African sea

Italian sea Sea of Spain France Greece Albania Roman sea inked handcrafted articulated sea fatigued never tired of setting forth Mediterranean

Then they brought us some mini pastries with tiny cassatas and cannoli and Santa Rosas and millefoglie and butter cookies and delicate little pastries and tarts with currants blueberries orange banana kiwi strawberry grapes almonds hazelnuts walnuts In the small secluded cafeteria the dust of ash and longing rose high The few diners were absorbed in their sacred repast The atmosphere was almost religious Everyone was absorbed in the transubstantiation of the meat and bread into human flesh and blood It was the miracle of the host repeating in that little corner of the world in the nineteenth-century space of the farmhouse outside of town with its big ostentatious courtyard surrounded by fields and granaries and the bustle of farmworkers with hoes and spades and tractors and bulldozers and bales of hay and grain piled in the pale sunshine of a bloody spring Blood flowed in rivers in the blood sky of lower Lombardy where cirruses and clouds of saints overlapped in a storm of longing that asked God for mercy compassion pleasure oblivion

On top of the tall Baroque hearths there was an array of tiny Baroque statuettes mirroring the statues we'd seen in the fields in an infinite echo It was the law of universal repetition whereby everything in the fractal geometry of the icosahedra of the sky is repeated thus giving birth to the succession of eternal generations that propagate on the earth in a circuitous and infinite formation Everywhere the architecture of sorrow is intertwined with the architecture of joy

Intertwined pleasure and pain radiated from our faces as the hostess brought wine meat and pastries She brought us a liver and potato pie made by baking in a golden crust pork ox lamb goat lamb mutton veal livers minced and mixed with butter thyme rum ricotta and béchamel interspersed with layers of potatoes with ricotta camembert prosciutto and fontina It was a golden timbale decorated with spirals and a little bread-dough cathedral I cut it with care and we watched that precious little Baroque structure collapse on the plate as happens with a building after the bombing of Hiroshima that reduces to ashes and dust and radioactive waste and diminished generations the human splendor and richness of the living world That splendor of food would transubstantiate inside us into the flesh of art and beauty of life

Through food pass flavor color heat scent and all the art of life that is enclosed in the hands of men and women who have the infinite ancient talent of cooking God is a cook Cooking is an art of God The gods feast on what God cooks every day creating immense cathedrals of bread and sugar crosses and stone metal cement palaces and bridges and gas stations and pastry and shortcrust and clouds of powdered sugar and children of ricotta milk and bread and women of butter and farmers of wheat and forests of pistachio pasta and rivers of water and wine and rum Every day and night God mixes the meat of creation with the glorious pulp of human flesh and chaos He stirs everything in the bitter chalice of the olive grove which contains centuries of ancient cuisine Cooking is an art of God

Absorbed in our sacred repast we bit into the thick liver drinking dense velvety wine We could feel the ox mutton sheep pig lamb viscera become the body of our body melding into creation in a sacred rapture of torment and torturous Baroque ecstasy of creation We were warm and filled with that great warmth of objects visions smells colors flavors We leaned back and drank more wine The nineteenth-century hall around us with its high vaulted ceiling sent vapors of fire into the sky

Outside the weather was darkening threatening thunder rain and storm The procession of saints was a black turbine of stone and longing pounded by violent blasts of water and wind The corn the wheat groaned in that furious heavenly interlude The Baroque storm swirled in vortexes of ice The monocular perspective of the small town was lashed and defeated by the flash storm Lightning bruised the turbulent sky All the architecture blurred in the small diluvial sky that beat down on the plains and fields of the Po Lowlands Violent thunder ripped through the distressed air All perspectives twisted in flashes of longing and cold The heat inside formed swirls of dust and smoke All the statuettes spun around in a surge of longing We listened to the rumble of the storm and thunder pounding on things and on men After an hour as the fire in the fireplace rose toward the roof of the world the storm subsided Patches of serene skies appeared between the clouds quieted by the hands of God

We got up We were sated with food and kisses The hostess kept bringing new patrons the list of her precious foods and Baroque dishes Out in the yard the grass and dirt smelled damp and fresh The dawn of a new morning rose over the world We walked over the blue-black stones of the long road with its systole and diastole of Renaissance and Baroque

We left the storm clouds behind and returned to the Pensione Certosa that awaited us with its quiet petit-bourgeois architecture embellished with silks wools brocades and flower vases We went up to room 53 where the shroud of sheets had been reassembled that morning Now the room seemed like a conventional space arranged with its flower vases and simple lines and furniture and dark-wood dressers We were still living in the food we had eaten The Baroque glory cried out inside us It was still cold out We lay naked under the blankets We gave each other little kisses Life was good We were happy Hand in hand we closed our desiring eyes

The next morning my head exploded into a thousand fragments of different sizes and colors The sky exploded over us We headed off down the long road of statues over which the icosahedra of the sky opened We followed the circumvolutions of the Baroque church through which we had passed the day before when the violent storm had shaken the bowels of the earth Now a faint sunshine spread happy and serene over the Lombard plain bathed in longing like Lucia lost in her mountains We stopped along the road to Monticelli where we returned the next evening to a small café stuck between the double row of Renaissance and Baroque buildings that pulsated with their rhythm of systoles and diastoles that made them the right and left sides of creation: the first rigid orthogonal infused with the torment of pain of one who is affixed to a cross at the meeting point between the abscissas of space and ordinates of time The other bound by love to the perpetual motion in which the harmony of chaos sings with its orgiastic dance of joy and pleasure We were enclosed within the beating heart of the entire universe Languid we looked at each other It was still a cold morning in a bloody April A light morning fog lay over the fields from which we could see the outline of the town behind the procession of stone statues that appeared slow and contorted beside the statues and the road where we were at the juncture of North and South Baroque and Renaissance pause and stillness time moving and time frozen in the scenic perfection of a Renaissance cube

We sat at a plain walnut table in a freezing room with high ceilings supported by stone architraves in a Renaissance house constructed according to the rigid logic of the architecture of pain that intertwined in the Baroque statuettes on the one lit fireplace that were the architecture of pleasure Our love was a delicious torture that defied the convictions of the Lombard petite bourgeoisie We asked for toast with butter and jam and shortbread cookies with chocolate and cream and milk and coffee and fruit: currants bananas apples oranges mandarins kiwi grapefruits and juices and mini ricotta and jam crostatas and sweet crepes filled with ricotta and chocolate with cream and honey with fruit and dusted with cocoa and powdered sugar We drank and ate knowing that we had placed ourselves on a very high mountain in defiance of social conventions We had taken on the burden of the challenge and carried it with honor In front of everyone I touched the rigid austere forms of Edda's South and the sinuous forms of Caterina's North They were the North and South of the world

After that breakfast we went out to see the sun shining soft and slow We had savored our food I knew that via food passes flavor color warmth scent and all of life's art contained in the hands of men and women who have the talent of age-old infinite cooking God is a cook Cooking is an art of God The gods feast on what God cooks every day creating immense pastry cathedrals and sugar crosses and buildings and bridges and gas stations and stone and metal and cement and short-crust pastry and puff pastry and clouds of powdered sugar and children of ricotta bread and milk and women of butter and farmers of wheat and forests of pistachio pasta and rivers of water wine and rum Every day and night God mixes the meat of creation with the glorious pulp of human flesh and chaos He stirs everything in the bitter chalice of the olive grove which contains centuries of ancient cuisine Cooking is an art of God

We hopped in the car to head back to Pavia to Belgioioso Castle where we enjoyed strolling through Renaissance and Baroque forms I took them to lunch in the restaurant built

into the castle's basement floor next to the border wall encircling the moat to defend the castle from enemies We ordered
pork with potatoes prepared by roasting a suckling pig over
an open fire sending circumvolutes of ash and smoke to the
ceiling-sky We asked for roasted potatoes and potatoes grilled
over coals dressed with oil thyme rosemary and pine nuts still
hot from the fire whose flames lapped the walls of its empty
hollow core Then we had them bring us fresh from the oven a
savory pie with ricotta béchamel peas spinach hard-boiled egg
and pork ciccioli that warmed the peaceful harbor of our love
We ordered hot chocolate to pour over a cake composed of
layers of shortcrust and sponge with rum-coffee cream filling
We washed it all down with liqueurs and hot coffee We went
outside and walked down the long road dividing the North and
South of the architecture of the world We felt like part of the
entire universe that persisted in its eternal motion of cosmic
systoles and diastoles that circumvolved eternally in volutes
of dust and smoke

We got in the car and followed the pale canals toward Pavia
which we traversed passing the station and the Renaissance
Baroque and Umbertine structures taking the road along the
Ticino River past which we again saw the long stone bridge
spanning the river with its shops and merchants of fabric and
jewels and baubles and shoes The landscape existed for itself
even without being seen We were happy to be in the world
without remainders without waste without regret without pain
without torment without obstacles and without tempests

We reached Pavia with its long rows of houses encircling
the big central piazza It was evening We were sated with life
I knew I didn't want to lock the stars the sky and God away in
a tower We stopped at a café to drink hot wine It was a warm
sangria with pineapple apple banana peach and rum I parked

on a street by the river We walked through the shops I gave
Edda and Caterina gray silk and wool skirts that slid soft over
Caterina's sumptuous and sinuous hips as she tried hers on
with childlike joy whereas the other fell in rigid pleats down
Edda's slender and angular southern shape They gave me a
scarf of silk and wool Then we went to a café to drink warm
wine Everywhere in the potbellied glasses and plates I saw
Baroque and Renaissance shapes Edda's eyes bore the traces
of the architecture of pain The locale was warm from the
oven vapors wafting out from the kitchen We ordered warm
broth mellowed with fontina and ricotta cheese Then veal
with tuna sauce and capers and olives and for warmth a side
of steamed vegetables with hot tartar sauce and mayonnaise
I was already thinking of the work that awaited me back in
the kitchen The thought of getting back to it didn't bother
me The future was without strife without worry or torment
or pain The thought of Tina's vacuum didn't disturb me After
dinner we got back on the road toward Monticelli We sped
down State Road 43 past canals poplars maples birches rice
fields At Caterina's cottage all was silent The dark sky lay in
its quiet The tractors were mastodons that slept in the store-
houses next to the barns and sheds and granaries On all the
wings of the big farm the shutters were closed Light peeked
out from behind just a few Perhaps some people were still
awake reading talking making love Caterina was happy but
uneasy at the thought of seeing her husband She re-entered her
realm of unquiet dust boredom and bonbons wrapped in the
soft skirt I had given her Another silence fell in the deserted
yard and behind her loomed the kingdom of tedium The door
closed behind her She vanished into the silent abyss of her
life I told her I would come back for dinner the next evening
The Amalfi Coast was so far away My roots sank in without

waste without remnants into the Padan Plain with its peace of flat and silent land

We kissed on the lips Edda and I drove back up to her isolated little house on her little hill that stood there like a cloistered nun's cell I kissed her mouth Her eyes were stern She was a woman living in the solitary space of death and of life which danced up high above us in the chaos of the celestial and infernal spheres I told her "Come to dinner tomorrow" She looked tranquil and grateful She disappeared into the secret and austere and glum darkness of her home

In the heart of the night I went back up to my house where my daughter slept like a ruddy-cheeked little girl in her room without ghosts without worries without terrors

The next morning I got up early and found Tina and my daughter in the kitchen drinking hot coffee and rum The breakfast table was set with care There was bread butter jam and cookies and coffee and pastries and croissants still warm from the oven They poured me some coffee

I'd already done my shopping for the evening Tina said she had a new man in her life Maybe she said it out of jealousy the same jealousy I saw in my daughter's eyes when I told her I had been out with Caterina and Edda

Tina went in her house and turned on the vacuum The infernal rumble left me distressed After breakfast with my daughter we put on simple housedresses and went back to the kitchen I stood with her and got to work for that evening preparing trays of casserole with lamb and ox and veal and chicken and pork and beef livers with alternating layers of liver and layers of ricotta mixed with béchamel and prosciutto and cheese with a splash of rum I covered them in pastry crust and spirals of ricotta béchamel and butter that melted soft and slow Separately I roasted carrots zucchini eggplant

plain and arranged them in serving plates with tartar sauce
Then I started to make dough for tagliatelle with egg flour
water butter and a dash of salt to dress it before serving with
the salmon béchamel that Edda and Caterina liked so much
I could see the jealousy in my daughter's sad eyes like those
of a little girl grown up before her time but we didn't speak
I continued kneading the pizza dough I'd made by mixing
water and flour with yeast I formed round and oblong fritters
and pan-fried them in butter and oil and dressed them with
tomato basil parmesan oil and ricotta I arranged them on a
Chinese porcelain plate I set them on the buffet which I had
decorated with cheese cellars and salt dough figurines I made
a long time ago Then I made some roasts: beef ox pork veal
goat mutton I placed them in the oval pans to bake with oil
and butter and rosemary sage and thyme I prepared myself
to receive the stone guests Slowly they came on the evening
of fog and crime in the Po Lowlands Then I prepared bread
baskets with bread of every shape and size round oblong with
olives with cumin with sesame with rosemary with Gaeta olives
white bread rye bread corn bread wheat bread from white flour
and yellow flour rice bread flatbread risen bread I set them on
silver plates and placed them on the tables On the buffet I had
prepared in crystal boats tartar sauce and mayonnaise and tuna
sauce and fruit bowls pineapple orange mandarin kiwi banana
currant strawberry apples peaches apricots and chocolate
cream and pastry cream with peaches and apricots on top I also
put little sandwiches with Olivier salad prosciutto and lettuce
tomato and ricotta and mayonnaise and butter and tuna and
Marie Rose sauce and shrimp As the entrée I brought a tray
of shrimp and scampi with rum-laced Marie Rose sauce and
capers and olives I looked out into the sky at the icosahedra
of heaven becoming part of the landscape of my dining hall

where the architecture of pleasure and joy and the architecture of sorrow and pain took shape that could be read everywhere in the world of humans who yearn for one another but cannot come together The Lombard landscape was silent with longing on the quiet evening where the glow of night was coming on The cutlery glittered It was the silver wedding gift I inherited from my mother who had passed down to me the angelic and infernal power of the ancient art of art and cooking

The women were dressed in bold colors with soft pleated robes in blue-violet Prussian blue indigo blue canary yellow sunshine orange pitch black cobalt green olive grass green red purple-red fire-blood-amaranth red celestial blue turtledove brown seagull gray hawk black-white robin black petrol green moss green earth brown They wore their matronly jewels reset and refurbished by the hairdressers and cosmeticians who had spread their colors across the faces of young old blond brunette women who strutted in their gaudy outfits They wanted to look like real ladies but were only Botero caricatures They leaned on the arms of their husbands and sons

The sparks from the oven crackled sending tongues of fire toward the sky of the ceiling The landscape was going mad trapped in the orgiastic longing that for the fourth time was exploding at Da Rosa The Lombard tycoons and arms traffickers and pushers with connections to the Sicilian mafia and the Neapolitan camorra and the Sicilian piovra They were pompous and wealthy bourgeois exposing their wealth to the eyes of all They were squeezed into tight slim-cut double-breasted blue suits that made them living mannequins in the orgiastic fires They whispered about my unconventional loves The men noticed my chest my hips getting rounder and rounder from food They wondered how a woman in her prime despite her age only yielded to other women They told one other that

I scorned the power of men They knew I preferred the peaceful harbor of lesbian love I thought of Edda and Caterina and taking them back to Vigevano I would calm my work anxieties I would get a break from the petit-bourgeois chatter that always hounds those who diverge from the flock recognizable under its charismatic leaders as the petite Padan bourgeoisie that spends its days in trade and commerce and feasting Aside from everything suppressed and repressed in life that was able to come out in this space Da Rosa was the only explosive point of their world They stopped talking about my life They unbuttoned their corsets and coats The women's stockings stretched thin over their plump legs They flaunted their breasts with cleavage bursting out of the chains of buttons that oppressed ample and ostentatious chests that had nursed babies like suckling pigs who once grown filled the fascist piazzas of Italy with shuttlecocks balls hoops and who in summer went to Cattolica where Botero's fat women like fat housebound hens wash dishes in winter and in summer fatten up like obscene pigs with little blond piglet children A fat tourism of office workers and wage slaves hanging off the magnificent winter towers of lifeguards in striped bathing costumes on deserted beaches populated by the infinitude of a thousand cabanas and identical blue-and-white-striped umbrellas like the tired pale color high in the Romagnan sky vast over the infinite sands The Adriatic coast is a gold mine of lost things And the rotund Botero women rest tired on their loves found and lost Their eyes lost in the void of industrial ennui Older mothers picked at heaping plates of pasta counting the slow rosary of their days Their laden bellies swollen with pain and regret Perhaps over their faraway children Young mothers big fat flabby and vulgar clucked like happy hens in a henhouse Blue and orange mixed with pink were the shades of the local kitsch

Cheap tacky shell souvenirs were displayed in streetside shops In Romagna fat men lean on the tired yet firm absolute and glorious plenitude of a metaphysical landscape like an empty fascist Italian piazza And the fat Tuscan hens pecked same as the Romagnan and the Neapolitan in the most beautiful gardens of Italy At the thought of their young the Neapolitan women bourgeois peasant proletariat servant housewives and wives to postal workers and rail employees felt their motherly blood boil in their veins Looking at the Cézannean bathers teenage sweethearts and rebel nuns the Neapolitan mothers felt the carnivalesque spirit of their lost childhoods embodied in the thousands of fat children crowding the magnificent long metaphysical beaches of Italy

And I looked at the others A number of onlookers surrounded us We laid aside everything that weighs us down and troubles us and haunts us We ran toward the mad summer that lay ahead of us with the long-fingered shadows of the tremendous Italian landscape Then the onlookers fell to the ground of the dust of time And time became a hallucinatory return among bags sandwiches suitcases and humans of all ages packed into a train station in a stifling heat Outside the train windows among smells of bananas and salami sandwiches the great slow Italian landscape slowly rolled past

They leaned over wide round hips as their bellies swelled in the firelight The sauces formed streams of caviar black and tomato red and tartar green and mayonnaise yellow and cocktail-sauce pink Flatbread and leavened bread descended into the stomachs of the insatiable West that locked its cravings inside a universe of nothingness that illumined in the evening where the deciduous queens of heaven traced fractal embroideries on the icosahedra of the sky Roasts passed from mouth to mouth They kissed shamelessly Touching breasts hips hands they passed morsels of food to one another as Caterina Edda and I had done so sweetly in our tribadic love where we were as kind and gentle as naiads and forest nymphs who didn't allow themselves to be distracted by Pan and the satyrs' violent advances who always play a paean to war on their panpipes to the women who divided fall into the concentration camps of male power but united defeat the orgy of planetary power Don't give anyone money—Ladies—or sell your soul to wars or the mafia or drug or arms traffickers or soul sellers like satyrs All over the planet wine flowed in rivers into throats parched by the fire crackling in the fireplace where the monachina pastries went up to the roof of the sky and the ceiling of the room that was a sky bent over the loves of the carnivalesque bourgeoisie of lower Padania A dog that was in the room riled up by the erotic tension pounced to bite a matron dressed in pearls and red brocade Silence fell in the room where the architecture of pain along with that of joy and of pleasure was being composed which are joined in the death and the life of creation of matter of nature of things and of men and of God who from the height of his throne watched the celestial and infernal angelic powers unleashed in the hall where the fourth feast was culminating The dog fell silent in the hall where war-weary warriors of night and heaven were unwinding in bodies exhausted by the ebullience of the fire and the wine and the food I had prepared with the ancient wisdom passed down to me from my mother's hands

The next day an abundant breakfast composed of muffins and pancakes served with maple syrup and apple juice and orange tangerine pear banana my mind shifted to the thought of the shopping I needed to do for the following day: lamb mutton chicken goat beef duck yellow and white flour eggs I left increasingly frequent intermissions between acts of work

Everywhere in shop windows in houses in pots and pans in glasses in offices I saw the form of the architecture of pain and pleasure within the harmony of chaos contained within the fractal geometry of the icosahedra of the sky I came to Edda's dark austere and severe building dressed in a simple black wool dress streaked with the color of the blood in her veins Her shape was outlined in the doorway of the grim stone house distantly encircled by rice fields brans granaries maples poplars birches canals She told me she enjoyed yesterday's dinner at Da Rosa but was sorry about the talk "We need to keep our love secret They don't understand They're too bound to convention" She was a beautiful fifty-year-old woman alone She was as thin as a tormented Giacometti with a head reduced to the dust of want and torment

The surrounding countryside stood quiet with frost and mist and fog and hidden crimes in the morbid heart of lower Padania which bears the marks of blood at the bottom Together we went to Caterina's husband's warehouses The tall Jugendstil structure rose with its blue plaster stone lined with rectangular and vertical decorations from which projected a bird a phoenix and a tragic mask from Greek theater Inside it was cold from the freezers full of meat and fish and the immense blocks of ice where the fish were stored: mullet sturgeon eel sweetbreads tellin clams salmon octopus that lay ardent with silver scales on bright green seaweed beds We bought kilos and kilos of peaches of meat of flour of eggs We haggled over the high price I told the seller if he didn't lower them I would go to the manager Then we went to Caterina's I had a heated argument with her husband about the prices of his goods He had as leverage my discretion in hiding my love I felt mocked by his vulgar expression I stopped arguing and let him seethe with jealousy He went back to his office and we went to Caterina's We knew he wouldn't object to the outing in front of the employees to keep tongues from wagging We found Caterina locked in her realm of unquiet dust In the room the pitchers and paintings bore the signs of a recent neglected past They were the legacy of the peasant and petit-bourgeois past of people who had only recently attained wealth Caterina was dressed in light brocade in the latest fashion from Milan Her husband bought her trinkets clothes furs jewelry from his travels so his precious plaything wouldn't betray him She had listened to the fight between her husband and me from her room She told me to be more careful so as not to stir up scandal

She carefully made herself up We kissed with Edda in the dusty penumbra of the room overlooking the yard where children playing ball hoop badminton and eating chocolate were called in by their mothers to do their homework Under the onlookers' prying eyes we set out for Pavia First we dropped the groceries at my house Later on the way we stopped at a restaurant outside the city where we asked for warm broth and salmon canapés We paid no heed to the expense We sat at a table after looking out the window from which we could see the plains lined with the embroidery of the branches that formed a lunar tangle of pale frost We asked for a pork loin roasted with butter oil rum rosemary sage and thyme Then we ate some sweet tarts and deli meats

A storm was about to break Warm with food and love we left for Vigevano We left the Pavia countryside with its rice fields and canals behind We reached Vigevano at dusk We returned to the Pensione Certosa where the maid from another era with a starched white apron and crinoline welcomed us It was a touch of domestic calm She didn't try to size us up She didn't bat an eye that we three women were again asking for one room

She showed us to room 42 in canary yellow and quartz gold It was a warm and inviting space for our love play We closed the door We took a hot shower Naked we slipped under the sheets Our hands searched for each other free away from home We shed our usual skin of lone women We molted off our fatigue or boredom or loneliness We ate cookies and chocolate making sure not to leave crumbs We looked out at the Lombard landscape of mist and crime in which a knife or a gun always lurked We got dressed and went down to dinner We ordered fresh tagliatelle carbonara tossed boiling hot with bacon pancetta prosciutto sausage ricotta and oil and raw egg blended and poured into a pan with the boiling pasta to combine Then we ate deli meats and sweets with coffee wine and punch

The next morning we came to a ghostly abandoned town once inhabited by peasants and farmers who had all left their ancestral trades to devote themselves to the oil mines that popped up copiously in the seventies But by decade's end the oil ran out triggering a slow exodus The peasants emigrated elsewhere We entered a decrepit house that shedded splinters that pierced our hands as we helped each other up the rickety stairs Upstairs there was an old credenza painted blue with childish designs next to a bed with an overturned mattress where the human humors that had inhabited it were still visible Everything was marked by neglect Downstairs there was a cutlery chest next to a peeling red wooden horse with little eyes gaping staring into space

Everywhere the signs of a past life were legible They appeared and reappeared in the objects the furniture the toys and the dishes Everywhere hands and their traces The landscape of past time extended like a veil over that which was no more Everywhere little laughs and shouts and whispers and voices inhabiting the atrocious and sacrificial silence of a time frozen on the clock of the past in the grim storm-frame of the ghostly landscape frozen on the clocks which were on the window grilles next to the geranium buds

We proceeded on our trip through the desolation We climbed some stairs that led to mezzanine floors where lay abandoned blankets with the signs of those who had abandoned them They were signs of sky earth sea that flew along with the icosahedra of heaven that rose up in a hosanna to creation The old oil wells were promontories for anteaters where the ants marched in formation like seven thousand horsemen climbing the stairs of heaven

After leaving the ruins and desolation we went back to the Pensione Certosa and made love We had the maid who was an English doll amid flowers and brocades bring us a tray of profiteroles and toast with jam and butter and pineapple currants blueberries oranges apples bananas strawberries and chocolate and cookies sprinkled with hazelnuts We exchanged kisses sweet with salt and sea We reached for one another and let ourselves be guided by our love

After two days I went back to Da Rosa and started cooking the roasts beef goat mutton ox lamb and rapini with garlic oil parmesan cheese and Caprese salads with friselle tomatoes oil salt and mozzarella After two days of work I took Edda and Caterina to the Maremma where horses run in the meadows of eternity and where fields of grain sickle into the cobalt and Prussian-blue sky while the deciduous queens of heaven became eternal in the forever of all eternity—Reader—I know that I sleep alone and when I die I'll bring my living and my dead all the struffoli tarts beignets savory pies fried pizzelle that I learned from my mother's age-old art I'll lay at the feet of the angels and God my roasts my stews broccoli pasta wine-braised sausages cassata roccocò mostaccioli pasta with ragù pasta with pesto sautéed vegetables stuffed chickens and turkeys hen in broth with celery carrot and potato stuffed suckling pig thrush with polenta rapini with garlic Olivier salad vitel tonnè shrimp cocktail green salad mayonnaise vegetables agrodolce stuffed peppers eggplant mushroom-style with tomatoes and garlic and eggplant-zucchini parmesan with mozzarella tomato and parmesan and roasted peppers in oil garlic and parsley meat-stuffed zucchini broth with butter fried chicken roasted chicken goose au gratin pork cutlets with rosemary-roasted potatoes and boiled potatoes and cannoli made with dough wrapped around metal tubes fried and filled with silky ricotta mixed with melted sugar candied fruit chocolate chips and wheat berries pastiera made with ricotta and orange blossom and sponge cake layered with pastry cream and chocolate cream I will lay at the feet of God and the feet of my living and my dead T-bone steaks and chicken cutlets and veal cutlets and sautéed beef liver with golden onions and grilled pork liver cooked in caul fat with rosemary thyme and sage browned in oil butter and onion and green bean potato salad and San Marzano tomato salad with anchovies salt oil parsley oregano olives and cubes of buffalo mozzarella and fresh mozzarella and margherita pizza and Camogliese pizza and puffed rice folded into chocolate honey rum and candied fruit and hazelnuts and almonds to make chewy torrone and rice pilaf and soufflé of onions potatoes tomatoes peppers and roasted eggplant and spaghetti with clams and carbonara with egg prosciutto and pancetta and bread with butter and sugar and bread with garlic oil and tomato and cocoa-dusted ricotta and Valtellina pizzoccheri blanched with potatoes spinach chard and dressed with butter oil parmesan sage thyme and bay leaf and cheese pies and crepes with marmalade and frittatas with vegetables with cheese and basil and pies with artichokes peas cabbage and potatoes baked in shortcrust and glorious Caprese cakes with almonds and rum and chocolate I will sit at the feet of the celestial thrones and offer the angels and demons and God Santa Rosa sfogliatelle and cannoli fried sheep brain and veal and artichokes and cabbage and golden-fried zucchini and trays of steamed artichokes with garlic and parsley and oil in their tender hearts and golden-fried artichokes and golden-fried zucchini and eggplant and roasted eggplant stuffed with pasta and meat and roasted eggplant stuffed with old bread mixed with water capers tomatoes cubes of mozzarella and parmesan until the breadcrumb surface turns golden and pieces of buffalo mozzarella in their glorious milk and rapini and rabe and rice balls with meat and ragù and peas and potato croquettes and shortbread cookies and beignets stuffed with meat and with pastry cream and the glory that is the Neapolitan pastiera with orange blossom-infused ricotta and cassata with pistachio and almond paste glaze candied fruit and ricotta and thousands upon thousands of trays filled with cakes made with layers of cream and glaze and chocolate and thousandfold millefoglie made by alternating layers of thin sheet pastry with layers of cream with butter and cream and powdered sugar and chocolate torrone made by pouring into molds chocolate almonds hazelnuts and whipped egg and pumpkin pasta and tagliolini in broth and in sauce and pappardelle and ravioli with walnut sauce and trofie with Ligurian pesto creamed with milk and meat ravioli and pumpkin ravioli and ravioli with cheese and ricotta and meat tagliolini in broth and spinach-ricotta ravioli in sage and butter and potato prosciutto mozzarella and cheese gateaux and thousands upon thousands of breaded mozzarellas and sautéed rabe and escarole pies made by stuffing trays of dough made with lightly sautéed escarole with pine nuts and raisins and a dash of salt and baked on low until golden brown and beef stew made by putting in cold water celery onion potato with shank bone and fat shoulder meat a piece of stew beef and all the spices thyme sage oregano parsley capers basil which are the glory of the Mediterranean garden and little plates of Brussels sprouts and cabbage dressed with ribbons of anchovy and sardines and parsley oil basil and green and black Gaeta olives and fried marinated anchovies and fried mozzarella and fresh mozzarella garnished with San Marzano tomatoes with garlic basil and oil and bread with butter and jam and bread with butter and sugar and bread with butter and tuna and cups of milk and cookies and malt and hard friselle softened in water and topped with diced fresh tomato and basil and oil and salt and mozzarella and fiordilatte and sugary fried doughnuts and buttery pastries and purees of meat and flour and vegetables or broth and fish I made for my daughter when she was a baby and little pastries made in the shape of little breasts or horns or golden hills and almond cookies and pasta casseroles and tur-keys with sausage-chestnut stuffing and other meats and ricotta and peas This will be my glory that I lay at the feet of God and the feet of my living and my dead I will fill with the pleasures of the belly the cosmos-sheet on which life is frescoed I will lay at God's feet my lone and infinite domesticitude in my cooking diffused under the skies of the Po Lowlands This has been my talent My God Love me God Love me for all eternity I have scattered the flavors and scents of my cooking across the world Accept my gift—Reader—I have fought my battle in life with food I've erected to the heavens cathedrals of pastry and baked longing and pleasure Accept my gift—Reader—I am only a woman I sleep alone Pause with me—Reader—in the suspended time of the eternal present in the land abandoned by God and men under the absolute immobile imploded light of things that exist even without being seen in the sea on the earth in the sky of God in the suspended time of the eternal present in infinite life

Pause with me—Reader—and look at the things that never end because the book of life, every book, is an infinite work and the cut of the frame is arbitrary like a painting of Pollock's

Like a pair of travel companions—Reader—let us linger on what never ends because life just as death has neither doors nor windows neither beginning nor end Death and life alike act together in a space-time where everything rotates and repeats according to the universal law of chaos and of repetition which according to Santayana is the only method of conserving the species And together we rest in the quiet dust of time in the land abandoned by God and men on the cosmos-sheet where life is frescoed in the imploded immobile absolute light of things that exist even without being seen in the sea on the land and in the sky of God

TRANSLATOR'S AFTERWORD

The Woman Who Had Visions

Marosia Castaldi was born in Naples in 1951 and passed away in Milan in 2019 at the age of sixty-eight. She was happy to be defined as a Neapolitan living in Milan, and her work embodies the conflict between North and South—in an interview, she once remarked that Naples was too beautiful: she needed to go to a place like Lombardy, flat, placid, gray, to be able to create. Rome might be famous for its ruins, but Naples—with its stratification of civilizations from undersea artifacts to nineteenth-century tombs, its visible mélange of cultural influences stretching back centuries, its dramatic geological and natural features—contains the pain of eternity, an eternity that is never realized—a metaphor for the world. Anyone who has spent any time in these places will grasp what she means, but it is a contrast that can be felt everywhere in her work, expressed in elemental, archetypal terms, landscapes that both mirror and mold the psyche.

I first came across Marosia's work not long after I myself moved to Milan. This novel, *La fame delle donne*, was included in a literary feature for the 2015 World Expo, hosted by Italy that year with the theme of food. A few weeks after I wrote her publisher, Agnese Manni, to inquire about translation rights, I received a phone call from Marosia herself, thus inaugurating our precious but all-too-brief acquaintance. I visited her a few times at her charming courtyard apartment in a *casa di ringhiera* at the storied address of Ripa di Porta Ticinese, on the canal right in the heart of Milanese nightlife that is the Navigli, where I would pass by wistfully after she was gone. Her novel *Il dio dei corpi* (The God of Bodies) begins with an autobiographical preface whose strangeness is heightened by its oblique relationship to the novel it precedes, which is about a tormented male artist taking care of an adopted child while trying to complete a project called "Eternity." The preface, titled "*Mentre scrivevo*" (best translated as "As I Lay Writing"), lucidly describes some of the personal background that reappears in her writing within the context of her hospitalizations due to anorexia, though she never names it as such. By the time we met, she was already consumed by the illness that eventually led to her demise—so slight, soft-spoken, gentle, that I could never quite picture her there among the crowds, though I know she lived a full life: an active childhood in Naples, degrees in philosophy and art, various travels, marriage and a move to Milan, raising two daughters, gallery exhibitions, teaching, lectures and literary events. As I knew her, she was completely open, eager, welcoming, unaffected—a magnanimous soul. Her philosophical education, her cultural background, and the small personal tragedies that mark any life led her to speak of "the soul" without irony, at once interrogatively and affirmatively, as the enigmatic but inalienable essence of people and things. She was an artist with such a painfully keen sense of inside and outside, the outside became absorbed into her rich inner life, haunted, tormented in its way, somehow uniquely in touch with the chaos of ur-being, what the philosophers describe as chora.

Marosia was a magmatic creator who left behind an extensive body of work. *La fame delle donne*, from 2012, is one of sixteen books in a career spanning from the 1980s through the 2010s. Punctuated with scattered essays, poems, and short stories, her major novels include *Per quante vite* (Feltrinelli, 1999), *Che chiamiamo anima* (Feltrinelli, 2002), *Dava fine alla tremenda notte,* (Feltrinelli, 2004), *Il dio dei corpi* (Sironi, 2006), and *Dentro le mie mani le tue. Tetralogia di Nightwater* (Feltrinelli, 2007). Her last novel, *La donna che aveva visioni* (Barbera, 2013)—The Woman Who Had Visions—contains elements of many of the former, as well as several passages that appeared previously in *The Hunger of Women.* The themes of her work are recursive: the interconnectedness of life and death, the metaphysicality of objects, the relationship between space and self, the trials of maternity and women's embodiment, explored in a range of styles and genres. It must be noted, however, that Castaldi is hardly a household name even in Italy, despite her productivity—the sort of writer who enjoys a respectable career but whose renown risks remaining incommensurate with their talent. When I asked the principal scholar of her work, Adalgisa Giorgio, why Castaldi wasn't read more widely, she simply replied that it was because her writing was difficult. In his preface to the monumental *Dentro le mie mani le tue. Tetralogia di Nightwater*, Domenico Starnone implored readers to pay attention to the book as if the fate of literature itself depended on it. Antonella Cilento, a writer and critic who runs a creative writing school where Marosia taught, wrote in her obituary for Castaldi that "the unremarked passing of so great a writer should make us reflect on the definitive victory of the market over literature." With her work's melding of autobiography, art, history, philosophy, and women's experience in a resolutely anti-realistic vein, it goes beyond the fantastic currents in Italian literature like Ortese or Calvino to find closer kin in international women writers: Virginia Woolf, Ingeborg Bachmann, Marie-Claire Blais, Clarice Lispector. But what is special about Marosia's work, beyond the surface timeliness of themes like maternity and love between women, is the exuberant Mediterraneanness animating it: ancient myth as expressions of a timeless unconscious, a deeply felt and theatrical sense of tragedy, the culture of a land and a people stretching back for millennia. Her Italy is syncretic, her Naples situated in Magna Graecia. Her use of repetition evokes Dionysian ritual practices where initiates would repeat the story of the god's killing and dismemberment by the Titans, a performative act whose recurrence was never identical and carried its speaker into another state. Devices that appear to be experimental are grounded in a profound classicism, bringing literature closer to the kind of aesthetic experience and subliminal pleasure we associate with music and song.

There is no denying that *The Hunger of Women* is a strange and difficult work, perhaps even more so in English. The first thing a reader will notice is that it has no periods, a constitutive feature of the Italian original that I have retained in English translation. What we have instead, as delimiters of sentence units, are initial capital letters, with context helping to resolve any momentary ambiguity. It is a technique that foregrounds beginnings over endings—origin is everything, it is the known, the past, and endings, our destination, our future, where a sentence may go, where a book will take us, is open. Spaces do all the work of creating pauses, without distinguishing between separation of word and sentence. *Panta rhei*, a stream of consciousness with few rocky impediments. For the second thing the reader—"Reader"—will notice is that the book is also extremely parsimonious where commas, colons, and other punctuation marks are concerned. If the general purpose of punctuation is clarity and pacing, what happens when we read a text virtually absent of those guideposts?

As Castaldi herself once wrote:

I've never used commas much. I tend to eliminate them: they are an obstacle. Of course they're necessary. There's always the issue of risking incomprehensibility. But they're not that necessary. Sometimes they are and sometimes they aren't. Anyway if in writing one didn't have the freedom not to have rules even when transgressing them, that is, the freedom not to turn transgression into rule, all writing would be an exercise in style and not a confrontation with the world. If a punctuation mark is abolished or used scarcely, if an unusually long space is placed between one word and another, if there are fifty paragraph breaks or none, it's because you want the page to *be*, not to represent, what you want to say. Writing can't circle around its object, it must forge it every time anew.

("Virgola debole" in *I segni. Punteggiatura*, ed. Alessandro Baricco et al., my trans.)

Of course, Marosia Castaldi writes in Italian, which boasts a syntactical flexibility that derives from its more heavily inflected Latin origins, so that lexical units could be said to evoke, spectrally, the case markers they no longer contain, arguably rendering punctuation less essential to comprehension as compared to English. Marosia's use of punctuation is nonetheless idiosyncratic, evoking a translingualism reminiscent of Benjamin's "pure language," a vocally-grounded expressiveness that seeks not to "circle around" but "forge": not to represent, but to *be*. It is this quality that led me to transpose Marosia's punctuation, where it appears, not uncritically or rigidly, but in keeping with the textual rhythm, the incantatory flow that constitutes the style of *The Hunger of Women*.

I could not possibly begin to enumerate the decisions that went into this translation, but will make a few comments to illuminate some of its difficulties. Rendering culinary terms is perennially thorny and readers' eyes may glaze over at the long lists of foods and recipes, many of which may be unfamiliar. Conventional wisdom has it that menu items are not to be translated, yet following such a precept in a literary work would have left intolerably lengthy sections of text in Italian. In this, I have erred on the side of anglicizing, drawing on extant cookbook terminology, for the sake of immediacy: being able to visualize what is being described without continually resorting to reference seemed more important than hyper-precision. Mediterranean ingredients, bacchanalian excess. At several points, Marosia uses a term I have translated as "domestic-itude," not the more immediately obvious "housewifery," for the Italian "casalinghitudine," a recent coinage from the 1987 novel by Claudia Sereni of the same name, meaning a condition of servitude to the domestic sphere in all its ambivalence. This is one node in her network of references, many of which are named outright, particularly those related to artworks, and others which are more subtle: Dante, Catullus, as well as some I have surely missed. No doubt another read of the Timaeus and the Neoplatonists would provide philosophical-cosmological context. I could not always account for the presence of a particular image and could only yield to the dream-logic of certain passages or words. Overall, musicality served as my lodestar, letting readability reside in the rhythm. Even a seemingly neutral phrase like "bassa Padania," a common term referring to the geographical region but which Marosia uses in all its metaphorical valence, rather than the top Wikipedia-equivalents of "Padan Plain" or "Po Valley" which are unknown outside the Italian context anyway, becomes the "Po Lowlands."

You cleave to style, as you must, but what is style? In an otherwise ponderous text, it might mean infusing levity for the sake of sound: "Aging's no picnic in the sticks" and not "Getting older in the provinces is hard." Translations are hybrids. Let them be monsters.

Marosia's work always challenged time, both the chronological structures of conventional narrative and the concept of clock-time with its indexical beginnings and clear full stops, and intermingled the living and the dead—because existence never ends, only changes, for eternity. Her life, and her death, were in her work, and my hope is to resurrect her, in my small way, here.

To be continued.

JAMIE RICHARDS
Milan–Los Angeles, 2023

Dear readers,

As well as relying on bookshop sales, And Other Stories relies on subscriptions from people like you for many of our books, whose stories other publishers often consider too risky to take on.

Our subscribers don't just make the books physically happen. They also help us approach booksellers, because we can demonstrate that our books already have readers and fans. And they give us the security to publish in line with our values, which are collaborative, imaginative and 'shamelessly literary'.

All of our subscribers:

- receive a first-edition copy of each of the books they subscribe to
- are thanked by name at the end of our subscriber-supported books
- receive little extras from us by way of thank you, for example: postcards created by our authors

BECOME A SUBSCRIBER,
OR GIVE A SUBSCRIPTION TO A FRIEND

Visit andotherstories.org/subscriptions to help make our books happen. You can subscribe to books we're in the process of making. To purchase books we have already published, we urge you to support your local or favourite bookshop and order directly from them – the often unsung heroes of publishing.

OTHER WAYS TO GET INVOLVED

If you'd like to know about upcoming events and reading groups (our foreign-language reading groups help us choose books to publish, for example) you can:

- join our mailing list at: andotherstories.org
- follow us on Twitter: @andothertweets
- join us on Facebook: facebook.com/AndOtherStoriesBooks
- admire our books on Instagram: @andotherpics
- follow our blog: andotherstories.org/ampersand

THIS BOOK WAS MADE POSSIBLE
THANKS TO THE SUPPORT OF

Aaron McEnery
Aaron Schneider
Abigail Walton
Adam Lenson
Ajay Sharma
Al Ullman
Alasdair Cross
Alastair Gillespie
Albert Puente
Alex Fleming
Alex Pearce
Alex Pheby
Alex Ramsey
Alexandra
  Stewart
Alexandra Webb
Alexandra
  Tammaro
Ali Ersahin
Ali Smith
Ali Usman
Alice Clarke
Alice Wilkinson
Alison Hardy
Aliya Rashid
Alyssa Rinaldi
Amado Floresca
Amaia Gabantxo
Amanda
Amanda Dalton
Amber Da
Amelia Dowe
Amitav Hajra
Amos
  Hintermann
Amy Benson
Amy Hatch
Amy Lloyd

Amy Sousa
Amy Tabb
Ana Novak
Andra Dusu
Andrea Barlien
Andrea Larsen
Andrea
  Oyarzabal
  Koppes
Andreas Zbinden
Andrew Marston
Andrew Martino
Andrew
  McCallum
Andrew Place
Andrew Place
Andrew Reece
Andrew Rego
Andrew Wright
Andrzej
  Walzchojnacki
Angelina Izzo
Angus Walker
Ann Morgan
Ann Rees
Anna French
Anna Gibson
Anna Hawthorne
Anna Kornilova
Anna Milsom
Anna Zaranko
Anne Edyvean
Anne
  Germanacos
Anne Kangley
Anne-Marie
  Renshaw
Anne Ryden

Anne Willborn
Annette
  Hamilton
Annette Volger
Annie
  McDermott
Anonymous
Anthony
  Fortenberry
Antonia Saske
Antony Pearce
Aoibheann
  McCann
April Hernandez
Archie Davies
Aron Trauring
Asako Serizawa
Ashleigh Sutton
Ashley Marshall
Audrey Holmes
Audrey Mash
Audrey Small
Barbara Mellor
Barbara Spicer
Barry Norton
Becky Cherriman
Becky
  Matthewson
Ben Buchwald
Ben Schofield
Ben Thornton
Ben Walter
Benjamin Judge
Benjamin Pester
Beth Heim de
  Bera
Betty Roberts
Beverley Thomas

Bianca Jackson
Bianca Winter
Bill Fletcher
Billy-Ray
  Belcourt
Bjørnar Djupevik
  Hagen
Blazej Jedras
Brandon Clar
Brenda Wrobel
Brendan Dunne
Briallen Hopper
Brian Anderson
Brian Byrne
Brian Isabelle
Brian Smith
Briana Sprague
Bridget Prentice
Briony Hey
Brittany Redgate
Brooks Williams
Buck Johnston
  & Camp
  Bosworth
Burkhard
  Fehsenfeld
Buzz Poole
Caitlin Halpern
Cameron Adams
Camilla Imperiali
Carla Ballin
Carla Castanos
Carole Hardy
Carole Parkhouse
Carolina Pineiro
Caroline Kim
Caroline
  Montanari

Dyanne Prinsen
Earl James
Ebba Tornérhielm
Ed Smith
Edward Champion
Ekaterina Beliakova
Elaine Rodrigues
Eleanor Maier
Eleanor Updegraff
Elif Aganoglu
Elina Zicmane
Eliza Mood
Elizabeth Braswell
Elizabeth Coombes
Elizabeth Draper
Elizabeth Franz
Elizabeth Guss
Elizabeth Leach
Elizabeth Seals
Elizabeth Sieminski
Elizabeth Rice
Ella Sabiduria
Ellen Agnew
Ellie Goddard
Emiliano Gomez
Emily Gladhart
Emily Paine
Emma Bielecki
Emma Louise Grove
Emma Morgan
Emma Post
Eric Anderson
Erin Cameron Allen

Erin Feeley
Ethan White
Evelyn Reis
Ewan Tant
Fawzia Kane
Fay Barrett
Felicity Le Quesne
Felix Valdivieso
Finbarr Farragher
Finn Brocklesby
Fiona Mozley
Fiona Wilson
Forrest Pelsue
Fran Sanderson
Frances Dinger
Frances Harvey
Frances Thiessen
Francesca Brooks
Francesca Rhydderch
Frank Pearson
Frank Rodrigues
Frank van Orsouw
Freddie Radford
Gala Copley
Gavin Aitchison
Gavin Collins
Gawain Espley
Gemma Hopkins
Geoff Thrower
Geoffrey Cohen
Geoffrey Urland
George Stanbury
George Wilkinson
Georgia Shomidie
Georgina Norton
Gerry Craddock
Gill Boag-Munroe

Gillian Grant
Gillian Spencer
Gillian Stern
Gina Filo
Gina Heathcote
Glen Bornais
Glenn Russell
Gloria Gunn
Gordon Cameron
Gosia Pennar
Grace Payne
Graham Blenkinsop
Graham R Foster
Grant Ray-Howett
Hadil Balzan
Halina Schiffman-Shilo
Hannah Freeman
Hannah Harford-Wright
Hannah Jane Lownsbrough
Hannah Rapley
Hannah Vidmark
Hans Lazda
Harriet Stiles
Haydon Spenceley
Heidi Gilhooly
Helen Alexander
Henrike Laehnemann
Holly Down
Howard Robinson
Hugh Shipley
Hyoung-Won Park

Iain Forsyth
Ian Betteridge
Ian McMillan
Ian Mond
Ian Randall
Ida Grochowska
Imogen Clarke
Ines Alfano
Inga Gaile
Irene Mansfield
Irina Tzanova
Isabella Garment
Isabella Weibrecht
Ivy Lin
JE Crispin
Jack Brown
Jacob Musser
Jacqueline Haskell
Jacqueline Lademann
Jacquelynn Williams
Jake Baldwinson
James Avery
James Beck
James Crossley
James Cubbon
James Higgs
James Kinsley
James Leonard
James Portlock
James Ruland
James Scudamore
James Silvestro
Jamie Mollart
Jan Hicks
Jane Dolman
Jane Leuchter
Jane Roberts
Jane Roberts

Jane Woollard
Janet Digby
Janis Carpenter
Janna Eastwood
Jasmine Gideon
Jason Bell
Jason Montano
Jason Sim
Jason Timermanis
Jeanne Guyon
Jeff Collins
Jeff Fesperman
Jen Hardwicke
Jenifer Logie
Jennifer Fain
Jennifer Fosket
Jennifer Mills
Jennifer Watts
Jennifer
  Yanoschak
Jenny Huth
Jenny McNally
Jeremy Koenig
Jeremy Sabol
Jerome Mersky
Jess Wood
Jesse Coleman
Jessica Gately
Jessica Laine
Jessica Queree
Jessica Weetch
Jethro Soutar
Jill Harrison
Jo Heinrich
Joan Dowgin
Joanna Luloff
Joanna
  Trachtenberg
Joao Pedro
  Bragatti
  Winckler
JoDee Brandon

Jodie Adams
Joe Huggins
Joel Swerdlow
Joelle Young
Johannes
  Holmqvist
Johannes Menzel
Johannes Georg
  Zipp
John Betteridge
John Bogg
John Carnahan
John Conway
John Gent
John Hodgson
John Kelly
John Miller
John Purser
John Reid
John Shadduck
John Shaw
John Steigerwald
John Walsh
John Whiteside
John Winkelman
John Wyatt
Jolene Smith
Jonathan Blaney
Jonathan Fiedler
Jonathan Harris
Jonathan Huston
Jonathan
  Paterson
Joni Chan
Jonny Kiehlmann
Jordana Carlin
Jorid Martinsen
Joseph Camilleri
Joseph Thomas
Josephine
  Glöckner
Josh Glitz

Josh Sumner
Joshua Briggs
Joshua Davis
Judith Gruet-
  Kaye
Judith Virginia
  Moffatt
Julia Foden
Julia Rochester
Julia Von Dem
  Knesebeck
Julie Atherton
Junius Hoffman
Jupiter Jones
Juraj Janik
Justine Sherwood
KL Ee
Kaarina Hollo
Kaja R Anker-
  Rasch
Kalina Rose
Kamaryn Norris
Karen Gilbert
Karen Mahinski
Karin Mckercher
Karl Chwe
Karl Kleinknecht
  & Monika
  Motylinska
Katarzyna
  Bartoszynska
Kate Beswick
Kate Carlton-
  Reditt
Kate Rizzo
Katharine
  Robbins
Katherine
  Sotejeff-Wilson
Kathrin Zander
Kathryn Burruss
Kathryn Edwards

Kathryn
  Williams
Katia Wengraf
Katie Brown
Katie Cooke
Katie Freeman
Katie Grant
Katy Robinson
Kavitha Buggana
Kay Cunningham
Keith Walker
Kelly Hydrick
Kelsey Grashoff
Ken Geniza
Kenneth Blythe
Kenneth
  Masloski
Kenneth Peabody
Kent McKernan
Kerry Broderick
Kerry Parke
Kevin Winter
Kieran Rollin
Kieron James
Kim Streets
Kris Ann Trimis
Kristen
  Tcherneshoff
Kristen Tracey
Kristy
  Richardson
Krystale
  Tremblay-Moll
Krystine Phelps
Kurt Navratil
Kyle Pienaar
Kyra Wilder
Lacy Wolfe
Lana Selby
Laura Ling
Laura Murphy
Laura Pugh

Laura Zlatos
Lauren Pout
Lauren
  Rosenfield
Lauren Trestler
Laurence
  Laluyaux
Lee Harbour
Leona Iosifidou
Liliana Lobato
Lilie Weaver
Lily Blacksell
Linda Jones
Linda Milam
Linda Whittle
Lindsay Attree
Lindsay Brammer
Lindsey Ford
Lindsey Harbour
Lisa Leahigh
Lisa Simpson
Liz Clifford
Liz Ladd
Lorna Bleach
Louise Evans
Louise Greenberg
Louise Jolliffe
Lucinda Smith
Lucy Huggett
Lucy Moffatt
Luise von Flotow
Luiz Cesar Peres
Luke Healey
Luke Murphy
Lydia Syson
Lynda Graham
Lyndia Thomas
Lynn Fung
Lynn Grant
Lynn Martin
Madden Aleia
Maeve Lambe

Maggie Humm
Maggie Livesey
Marco
  Medjimorec
Margaret Dillow
Mari-Liis
  Calloway
Maria Ahnhem
  Farrar
Maria Lomunno
Maria Losada
Marijana Rimac
Marina
  Castledine
Marion
  Pennicuik
Marja S
  Laaksonen
Mark Bridgman
Mark Reynolds
Mark Sargent
Mark Sheets
Mark Sztyber
Mark Tronco
Mark Troop
Mark Waters
Martha W Hood
Martin Brown
Martin Price
Martin Eric
  Rodgers
Mary Addonizio
Mary Clarke
Mary Heiss
Mary Tinebinal
Mary Wang
Maryse Meijer
Mathieu Trudeau
Matt Davies
Matthew Cooke
Matthew
  Crossan

Matthew
  Eatough
Matthew Francis
Matthew Gill
Matthew Lowe
Matthew
  Woodman
Matthias
  Rosenberg
Max Cairnduff
Max Longman
Maxwell
  Mankoff
Maya Feile
  Tomes
Meaghan
  Delahunt
Meg Lovelock
Megan Taylor
Megan Wittling
Mei-Ting Belle
  Huang
Mel Pryor
Melanie Stray
Melissa Beck
Melissa
  Quignon-Finch
Michael Aguilar
Michael Bichko
Michael Bittner
Michael Boog
Michael Eades
Michael James
  Eastwood
Michael Floyd
Michael Gavin
Michael Parsons
Michele
  Whitfeld
Michelle
  Mercaldo
Miguel Head

Mike Abram
Mike Schneider
Miles Smith-
  Morris
Mim Lucy
Molly Foster
Mona Arshi
Morayma
  Jimenez
Moriah Haefner
Nancy Garruba
Nancy Jacobson
Nancy Langfeldt
Nancy Oakes
Nancy Peters
Naomi Morauf
Nargis McCarthy
Nasiera
  Foflonker
Natalie Ricks
Nathalie Teitler
Nathan
  McNamara
Nathan Weida
Niamh Thompson
Nichola Smalley
Nicholas Brown
Nicholas Jowett
Nicholas
  Rutherford
Nick James
Nick Marshall
Nick Nelson &
  Rachel Eley
Nick Sidwell
Nick Twemlow
Nicola Hart
Nicola Sandiford
Nicolas Sampson
Nicole Matteini
Nicoletta
  Asciuto

Silje Bergum Kinsten
Simak Ali
Simon Clark
Simon Pitney
Simon Robertson
Sophie Nappert
ST Dabbagh
Stacy Rodgers
Stefano Mula
Stephan Eggum
Stephanie Miller
Stephanie Smee
Stephanie Wasek
Stephen Fuller
Stephen Pearsall
Stephen Yates
Steve Clough
Steve Dearden
Steve Tuffnell
Steven Norton
Steven Williams
Stewart Eastham
Stuart Wilkinson
Sujani Reddy
Susan Edsall
Susan Ferguson

Susan Jaken
Susan Wachowski
Susan Winter
Suzanne and Nick Davies
Suzanne Kirkham
Tania Hershman
Tara Roman
Tatjana Soli
Tatyana Reshetnik
Teresa Werner
Tess Cohen
Tess Lewis
Tess Lewis
The Mighty Douche Softball Team
Theo Voortman
Thom Keep
Thomas Alt
Thomas Fritz
Thomas van den Bout
Tiffany Lehr
Tim Kelly

Tim Scott
Timothy Cummins
Tina Rotherham-Winqvist
Tina Juul Møller
Toby Ryan
Tom Darby
Tom Doyle
Tom Franklin
Tom Gray
Tom McAllister
Tom Stafford
Tom Whatmore
Trevor Latimer
Trevor Wald
Tricia Durdey
Turner Docherty
Val & Tom Flechtner
Vanessa Baird
Vanessa Dodd
Vanessa Fernandez Greene
Vanessa Heggie
Vanessa Nolan
Vanessa Rush

Veronica Barnsley
Victor Meadowcroft
Victor Saouma
Victoria Goodbody
Victoria Osborne
Vijay Pattisapu
Wendy Langridge
William Brockenborough
William Leibovici
William Mackenzie
William Orton
William Richard
William Schwaber
William Wilson
Yoora Yi Tenen
Zachary Maricondia
Zoe Taylor
Zoë Brasier